THE HOUSE ON HACKMAN'S HILL

Joan Lowery Nixon

AN
APPLE®
PAPERBACK

SCHOLASTIC INC.
New York Toronto London Auckland Sydney

ISBN 0-590-33804-8

Copyright © 1985 by Joan Lowery Nixon. All rights reserved. Published by Scholastic Inc.

12 11 10 9 8 7 6 5 4 3 2 1   3   6 7 8 9/8 0 1/9

Printed in the U.S.A.   11

PART ONE:
THE MUMMY'S CURSE

1

We're going to find a mummy," Jeff said. He came to a stop so abruptly that his cousin Debbie bumped into him, kicking snow against his leg and down the top of his boots.

"Very funny," she said. She brushed snow from the top of her camera case. "I suppose we'll find him hopping down the road in the snow. You know, that's why I never liked those old movies with mummies walking after people, because their legs are wrapped together, and — "

"I'm not kidding," Jeff said. "Last time I was here visiting Grandma and Grandpa I found out there's an old deserted house near here that's supposed to have a mummy hidden somewhere inside it, and there's a ten-thousand-dollar reward for anyone who finds the mummy! Think about it, Debbie. We could get that reward!"

Debbie looked suspicious. "Grandma and Grandpa have never said a word about a house with a mummy in it."

"I know. They don't like to talk about it. I heard the story about the mummy from their neighbor, Mr. Karsten."

"Old Mr. Karsten? C'mon, Jeff. He was just kidding you."

"No, he wasn't," Jeff said. "He told me that sometime, when we could sit down and talk about it, he'd tell me the whole story. At least he told me where the house is."

"Did you look for the mummy?"

"Nope. I knew we'd both be here during early spring break so I waited for you. I thought you'd want to hunt for the mummy with me."

"Ha! You mean you were too scared to go into the house by yourself!"

"Well," Jeff admitted, "looking for a missing mummy is not really something I want to do all alone."

Debbie grinned at him. "Okay, oh brave and mighty mummy-hunter. Where is this house?"

Jeff grinned back. He was glad he and Debbie had been invited to visit Grandpa and Grandma at the same time. Since their families now lived in different parts of the country they didn't often have the chance to get together. Twelve years ago Debbie and Jeff had been born just two weeks apart and had been friends since they were old enough to dump their cereal on each other's heads.

They even looked a lot alike, with their red hair and freckles. "The gruesome twosome," Debbie's big brother, Don, always called them; and Jeff's mother sometimes sighed and said, "I don't know how the two of you can get into so much mischief every time you get together!"

But finding a mummy wouldn't be called "mischief," especially when he and Debbie collected that big reward. "The house is up here," Jeff said. "I discovered it last summer." He waded through the drifts at the side of the road and began to climb upward, grabbing at the snow-covered shrubs for handholds.

"How far is it?" Debbie asked, as she began to climb after him. "The sun will be going down pretty soon, and this is a lonely place to be caught in the dark!"

"It won't take long," Jeff said.

He began to climb farther, finding it easier going now. Behind him he heard the crack of twigs as Debbie called, "Hey, wait for me. I'm coming, too."

The strip of forest was narrow, and Jeff and Debbie soon found themselves standing at the edge of a wide clearing. They looked up to see a huge brick house on the crown of the hill, its glowing windows reflecting the setting sun. It was a strangely designed house, with towers and turrets and sagging balconies. Gigantic pillars stood on the porch like sentries at each side of the massive front door. The porch steps were broken and so were some of the windows.

"I'm going to get a picture of that," Debbie said, quickly tugging her camera out of the case. "We're having a contest in our camera club at school, and I want to win."

She aimed, and the camera whirred as the photograph rolled out.

"I thought you had to have an expensive camera to win contests," Jeff said. "How can you hope to win if you're taking pictures with a quick-shot camera?"

"There's a category for photographs taken with this kind of camera," Debbie said. She studied the picture as it began to take shape. "Hmmm — pretty good." She put the camera and photograph into the case, adding, "I just might buy an expensive camera with my half of the reward money we'll get for finding the mummy. What are you going to do with your half?"

Jeff shrugged. "Oh, I don't know. Maybe I'll give it to my father." Of course Debbie knew that Jeff's father had gone to Texas to look for another job after the company he had been with for years and years had suddenly been sold. But she didn't know how tired his father had looked and how his mother seemed to worry all the time. The reward for

6

finding the mummy would be his way to help, and Jeff was eager to start.

A sudden puff of wind shook a branch near their heads, and a glob of snow fell next to them with a loud plop. Debbie shivered. "You told me the house was deserted, but I think you're wrong. Somebody must live there."

"Mr. Karsten said the house has been empty for years."

"But somebody in that house is watching us. I feel it. Don't you? And I don't think he wants us here."

"I don't see anybody," Jeff said, but he had felt it, too, the odd sensation that someone was staring at them from behind one of those gleaming windows. So he allowed Debbie to pull him back into the shelter of the trees.

"That place is creepy," Debbie said, as she slipped and stumbled down to the road. "Let's ask Grandma and Grandpa what they know about it."

"I told you," Jeff said, "they don't want to talk about it."

Jeff was right. As they burst through the back door of their grandparents' house, Debbie said, "We saw this creepy old house up on the hill, Grandma. Tell us about it."

"Get out of those wet clothes first," Grandma said, helping Debbie tug off her gloves. "I've made beef stew for supper, and a big bowl of that will warm you up."

Jeff and Debbie left their boots and coats on the service porch and followed Grandma into the kitchen that was warm with the fragrance of freshly baked rolls and simmering stew.

Grandpa ladled chunks of beef and potatoes and golden carrots from a large china tureen. "I know you're hungry after your walk," he said.

Jeff was hungry, but he was also curious. Before he took a bite he asked, "Tell us about that strange old house on the hill."

"You must mean the house on Hackman's Hill," Grandpa answered. Grandma gave Grandpa a sharp look, and he added, "It's just an old house. You wouldn't be interested in it."

"Why don't you want to tell us about the house?" Jeff asked. "Mr. Karsten told me something about it the last time I was here."

"Have one of these nice, warm, homemade rolls, Jeff," Grandma said.

Debbie suddenly put down the roll she had buttered. "I know," she said. "That house is supposed to be haunted or something, isn't it, just because there's a mummy in it? That's why you don't want to talk about it."

Grandma sighed. "Everyone in town has heard silly rumors about Hackman's Hill, but that's all they are — rumors. And I don't believe in spreading rumors. Whatever took place there happened so long ago that I doubt if anyone in town is old enough to remember the real story. Now enjoy your dinner but save some room, because I made apple dumplings for dessert."

Debbie glanced at Jeff, and he knew she was thinking the same thing he was. There *was* someone who was old enough to remember the real story. Mr. Karsten! He'd be glad to tell them!

Early the next morning, after they had helped with the breakfast dishes, Jeff and Debbie put on their boots, gloves, caps, and scarves, and made their way across the street to Mr. Karsten's front door.

He opened it as soon as they knocked, almost as though he had known they were coming and knew what was on their minds. Mr. Karsten was as bent and knobby as a limb from an apple tree, and his bright eyes peered out from a face as wrinkled as an apple left too long in the sun. He stood aside so they could file into a living room that was dimly lit with only a yellowed light that filtered through a dried and tattered lamp shade.

Mr. Karsten's face crinkled into a broad smile. "As soon as you've taken off your outside things and hung them on that rack by the door, I'll be ready to tell you about the house on Hackman's Hill."

Debbie gasped, and Jeff stammered, "How did

you know we were going to ask you about the house?"

"I knew you were eager to hear the whole story about the house," Mr. Karsten said. "Besides, I saw what direction you took on your walk yesterday afternoon."

"It's a weird place," Debbie said. She tugged off her coat and gloves, and shoved them onto the coatrack. "Jeff told me that no one lives in the house, but I think he must be wrong."

"No one lives in the Hackman house," Mr. Karsten said. "No one has dared set foot inside that house for many, many years."

"We felt like someone in the house was watching us," Jeff said.

Mr. Karsten paused before he answered, "You may have been watched, all right. But if so, it wasn't by a living human being."

"Then what was it?" Debbie whispered.

"I'll tell you about the house," he said. "Please sit down and make yourselves comfortable." He pointed to an overstuffed sofa. As Jeff and Debbie perched there he slowly lowered himself into a lumpy armchair and leaned toward them.

Jeff held his breath as Mr. Karsten quietly said, "I can tell you the true story, because long ago I was there with the horror on Hackman's Hill."

2

It was in the year 1911, two years after my father died, that my mother brought me to live in Dr. Hackman's house," Mr. Karsten said. "Mother had been doing secretarial work in the history department at the university. That's where she met Dr. Hackman. He was a peculiar man, sometimes pleasant enough, but sometimes very rude and gruff." He paused and added, "Sometimes even cruel. He was always pleasant to Mother, though. He seemed to like her very much. But he hated children, and therefore he hated me. I always had the feeling he wished I didn't exist."

"I bet everybody hated him," Debbie said.

"As to what people thought of him personally, I don't know. In his profession Dr. Hackman was a respected, well-known professor of history, who specialized in Egyptian studies. He planned to retire from teaching and spend his remaining years cataloguing his papers and his valuable collection of artifacts."

"Is that where the mummy comes in?" Debbie asked.

"Be quiet!" Jeff said, poking her with his elbow. "You're interrupting the story."

But Mr. Karsten just smiled and continued.

To my dismay Mother accepted the position of Dr. Hackman's secretary, and we moved our few belongings to the big house on Hackman's Hill. I was twelve years old, and I'll never forget my feelings of dread as I stood on the porch of that massive house, so shut away from the rest of the world. The sun was beginning to set, and the windows of the house caught its rays, gleaming so brightly in reds and golds it seemed as though the house was lit with an inner fire. The driver of the cart that had brought us from the train depot had not stayed to carry in our bags. He had driven his horse and cart along the road to the rear of the house with a large packing case for Dr. Hackman and two passengers who seemed to be delivering the crate. They were small men who kept to themselves. When they spoke to each other it was in a language I had never heard.

The crate had come on the same train as we had, the men apparently riding in the baggage section with it, and I wondered what could be in it. The box was as long as a tall man and about three feet wide and three feet deep.

12

No one had come from Dr. Hackman's house to greet us. My mother held my hand tightly, as we waited for someone to answer the deep clang of the bell pull, so I'm sure she was a little frightened, too.

"It's all right, Paul," she whispered to me. "This is going to be a good home for us for the next few years, and my salary will pay for your college education." It was Dr. Karsten's grand offer of three thousand dollars a year that made my mother accept the job. She would never be able to make that much at the university.

Just then the door swung wide, and a tall, thin man bowed to us.

Mother looked up at him and said, "I'm Mrs. Karsten, and this is my son, Paul. Will you please inform Dr. Hackman we have arrived?"

Before the man could answer, Dr. Hackman stepped around him. He was short and pudgy with a curly, gray beard and was wearing a dark suit and vest, a striped shirt with a starched collar, and a tie. Topping his outfit was a blue yachting cap like the one worn by the wealthy Commodore Vanderbilt. On the few times I had seen Dr. Hackman at the university he had worn that yachting cap. Mother had explained that it was an odd superstition with him. "His good-luck cap," she had said, reminding me there was no truth in the so-called power of good-luck charms.

But Dr. Hackman's blue cap fascinated me as he bounced onto the porch, tipped his cap to Mother, and said, "Good to see you, Mrs. Karsten. Sorry to keep you waiting. I had to attend to a delivery at the back door. The men have left now." He ignored me. "I trust the trip was a pleasant one?"

"It was quite pleasant," Mother said.

I immediately pulled off my cap and said, "Good day, sir."

Dr. Hackman merely grunted in my direction, then said to Mother, "I see you've met Jules. As soon as you are settled, I'll introduce you to his wife, Anna. They do a fine job of taking care of the house for me." Mother must have looked surprised, because he added, "Oh, I know the house is quite large, but most of it is used for storage of my papers and artifacts. We live in only a few rooms, and those are easily cared for. Now come in, come in!"

The door shut out the sunlight, and I blinked, trying to become accustomed to the dim entry hall. Except for the electric lights that must have been added recently, the room looked like something from an old castle. Tapestries and paintings hung on the walls between ornate sconces that held bare light bulbs, and a large, round table in the center of the room was cluttered with small bowls, jars, and statues. One of the statues, which stood in the middle of the table, was taller than the others. It had the body of a human but the head of some kind of animal. I wanted to examine the statues, but at the same time I wanted to stay as far away from them as possible.

Opposite the front door was an open archway leading into a hallway. The arch was framed in wide oak beams. There were words deeply carved into the top beam, and I moved closer in order to read them, whispering them aloud: "ONLY I KNOW THE SECRET."

Dr. Hackman chuckled, and I turned to see that he had been watching me. "You're wondering what that means? Well, Paul, it wouldn't be a secret if you knew, would it? Oh, I have many, many secrets!" He motioned to Jules. "Bring the luggage, Jules. I'll lead the way." Dr. Hackman ushered us into a room that was across from the head of the stairs.

It was about as cheerful as any room in that house could be. Heavy swags of dark-green velvet draperies hung over the windows, shutting out most of the light. The bed, chest, and wardrobe were elegant, and there were fringed pillows and things ladies would like.

"I hope this meets with your satisfaction, Mrs. Karsten." Dr. Hackman looked pleased with himself. He knew this room was far nicer than the small rooms we had rented near the university.

"Thank you. It's lovely," Mother said. She eyed the draperies in such a way I knew she would pull them back and let in the light as soon as possible.

"Then we'll leave you to unpack," he said. "Dinner will be at seven, and you may rest until then. We won't begin work until tomorrow morning."

He put a firm hand on my shoulder. "Paul," he said, "I'll let Jules take you upstairs to your room."

For a moment I was as frightened as though I were a small child. "You mean my room won't be near Mother's?" I blurted out, then wished I could swallow the words as they all stared at me.

"I thought you'd enjoy a room in one of the towers," Dr. Hackman said. "It's a fine room for a boy. It has a good view of the valley, and a narrow, winding staircase that I would have enjoyed when I was young."

I gulped and nodded, confused by his seeming friendliness, and even more embarrassed because I was blushing. "I'm sure I'll like it, sir," I managed to say, and I followed Jules to the end of the corridor, through a small door at the back of the house, and up a narrow, twisting stair to another door. Jules surprised me by pulling a key from his pocket and unlocking the door.

"Why was this room locked?" I spoke my thoughts aloud, as I wondered why a room so secluded should be locked when other rooms in the house obviously were not.

"I do not know," Jules said. "My job is to simply follow Dr. Hackman's orders." He opened the door and stepped into the room ahead of me.

My first reaction was gratitude that it wasn't a heavily decorated room like Mother's. There was a narrow bed that looked comfortable enough, a plain desk and chair, an old wardrobe and chest of drawers, and a lamp with a pleated silk shade and gold fringe. While two of the walls were straight and at right angles, the other two walls blended into each other in a wide curve, and on that curve were three large windows.

I walked to the middle window, which was open. I gasped as I looked down to jagged rocks and the valley floor far below.

"This room is on the edge of a cliff!" I shouted.

Jules nodded, and for the first time he spoke. "Be very careful. The window sills are low. Another accident would be unfortunate."

I shut the window and backed away. "What do you mean? Did an accident happen here?"

"I should not have said what I did. It is not my place." Jules put down my luggage, put the key on top of the chest of drawers, closed the door, and was gone before I could ask what he meant.

It took only a short time to put away my clothes and few possessions. I had brought two books and some pencils, and I tossed them into the top drawer of the chest. One of the pencils bounced against the edge of the drawer and flew behind the chest. I got down on my knees and wiggled my fingers behind the chest until I managed to reach it. But I had touched something else — something hard and cold. I used the pencil to work it out and examined it.

In my hand was a triangular-shaped piece of metal that was as thin and small as a coin and looked as though it might be gold. There were odd scratchings around the edges on both sides. On one side was a design that looked like a pair of eyes. On the other seemed to be an animal head. Maybe Dr. Hackman would know what it was. I dropped it into my pocket to show to him later. I felt very uncomfortable here. I wondered if Mother felt the same.

Well, I thought, it would soon be dark, and perhaps I could discover more about this place that was my new home. I went quickly down my narrow stairway and followed the hallway on the second floor to the grand staircase. No one was in sight, so I walked downstairs, pausing for another quick look at the table with the strange statues, crossed the hallway, and entered the large parlor. It was cluttered with all sorts of large, deep chairs, tables and fringed tablecloths covered with objects, many of which seemed to be Egyptian in origin. But on one table was a record player with a large horn on top and a crank on the side. Next to it was a stereoscopic viewer and slides. Paintings and hangings nearly covered the walls.

The room on the other side of the hallway was a library. Next to that was an office of some sort and a desk piled high with a scramble of papers. A telephone with a crank on one side was on the wall behind the desk.

I passed a dining room and walked into a kitchen that was strangely empty, although the room was warm from a huge wood-burning stove on which an enameled pot of something bubbled and steamed. At the far end of the kitchen, past the wooden ice box, a door was ajar, and I went through it. Perhaps Anna was there and I could introduce myself.

But I was still alone. I found myself in a wide, closed-in porch. Cleaning tools were against one wall, along with countless boxes and bottles and barrels. But what interested me most was the large packing crate that rested against the wall. I recognized it as the one that had come with us from the depot.

The temptation was too great to resist. I saw that the nails that had held the lid shut had been removed. I had to see what was inside that crate.

I squatted next to the crate. Slowly, carefully, trying not to make a sound, I began to lift the lid. But suddenly something gripped my shoulders, and with a shout I fell backward.

3

I yelped again as I sat on the floor with a thump. A voice growled in my ears, "Be quiet, boy! Now get to your feet!"

I scrambled and stumbled and found myself facing Jules and a plump woman whose hands were tucked under her long, white apron. She scowled at me and spoke to her husband. "This is the boy the doctor has brought here?"

"Yes," Jules said.

"I'm Paul Karsten," I hurried to tell her. I quickly tried to dust off the knees of my knickers and tuck in my shirttail so I'd seem more presentable. "I'm very happy to meet you," I added.

"Happy? In this house?" She shrugged. "I suppose you're hungry. Boys are always hungry."

"Yes, ma'am," I said, suddenly realizing it had been a long time since I had eaten a full meal.

"Come with me," she said, but Jules held up a hand.

"First, there is something Paul should know."

He put his hands on my shoulders again, this time facing me. "Dr. Hackman's property in this house is not to be touched, except at his invitation. Many of his things are valuable and would be easy to break. Do you understand?"

"Yes," I said. I couldn't help glancing at the wooden crate.

Jules shook his head. "If Dr. Hackman wants you to know what arrived in that crate, he will tell you."

He turned me toward the kitchen, and I meekly followed Anna. She handed me an apple and a wedge of sharp, yellow cheese. "Dinner will be in another hour," she said. "This should hold you until then."

"I didn't mean to make Jules angry," I murmured.

She rested one hand on my shoulder. "Jules is not angry," she said. "He is a good man, and he is just trying hard to do a good job." She sighed and shook her head. "This is not the right place for a young boy to come to."

It was rapidly growing dark, and Anna turned on the overhead light. It swung from its chain, causing shadows to jump and leap across the room. As quickly as I could I ate the apple and cheese, thanked Anna, and hurried from the kitchen. I wanted to talk with my mother.

Bulbs were lit in the hallway, and the parlor was

lighted, although no one was there. I rushed through the entry hall and up the stairs, knocking loudly at the door to Mother's room.

She quickly opened it. "My goodness, Paul!" she said. "What is disturbing you?"

I realized that my face was hot and I was breathing rapidly. I squeezed past her into the room and said, "I don't like this place, Mother. I think we should leave."

She had changed to a fresh shirtwaist with balloon sleeves and a small tie and a plain serge skirt that swept the floor. Her face, scrubbed clean from the grime of our travels, shone, and I thought what a fine-looking woman my mother was. She didn't fit in this strange house, and neither did I.

It took all my courage, and I could feel my face grow even warmer as I stammered, "This house frightens me. And so do the people in it."

Mother looked surprised. She perched on a little purple armchair and motioned to me to come to her. She had already unpacked, and the familiar sight of her hatpins stuck into their fat, red pincushion, and her crystal perfume atomizer made me feel somewhat better. Mother took my hands and smiled into my eyes. "Dear Paul," she said, "now I understand. This is an unusual home, because part of it must look to you like the museum your father and I took you to visit in the city."

I nodded, and she went on. "I should have remembered how the Egyptian room frightened you. But you were just a little boy then, and it never occurred to me that you would still be afraid."

"I don't mean to be afraid," I said, as I tried to stand straighter and taller. "But those awful statues downstairs, especially the one that looks like a man with an animal's head, and those strange paintings where people look like their legs are on sideways...." I couldn't finish the sentence.

I was glad that Mother didn't laugh. She nodded as though she was thinking about what I had said and finally answered. "Those are art objects from a people who lived many, many years ago. Their art was more primitive than ours. They expressed what they saw in very different ways. It may seem strange and a little frightening to you now, but to them it was beautiful and right."

"Why does one of the statues have an animal head? There weren't any people like that around then, were there?"

"It's a symbol, representing a god, that's all. Of course there weren't people who looked like that."

"I still wish we were home," I mumbled.

Mother hugged me. "Life has many changes for us, not all of them what we'd choose, but we must do our best."

Her voice was suddenly sad, and I knew how

much she must miss my father. I didn't want to make life harder for her, so I quickly answered, "I'm all right now. Everything will be fine."

A bell rang in the entry hall. "That must be the call for our evening meal," she said. She hugged me again and got to her feet, smiling. "Will you take me down to dinner, sir?"

I laughed and gave Mother my arm. We walked down the stairs, still smiling, and saw Dr. Hackman watching us.

"How very nice to see that you are quickly adjusting to your new home," he said.

I took a deep breath. "Dr. Hackman," I said, "this afternoon I looked through some of the rooms downstairs. I went onto the back porch, where I saw the crate that arrived here when we did. I was curious and wanted to look inside, but Jules stopped me in time. I wish to apologize for my curiosity, sir."

Mother's hand tightened on my arm, but Dr. Hackman game a peculiar chuckle. "It was honorable of you to tell me this, Paul." He rubbed his beard, thought for a moment, then said, "I'm afraid that you will have to confine yourself to your own room and to the living areas that I do not lock. There are many rooms in this house that, because they contain valuable parts of my collection, I'll ask you never to enter."

"Yes, sir."

24

"However, life here won't be so bad. I do have some interesting things to show you. Very interesting things." His voice was solemn, but there was a twinkle in his eyes that puzzled me. He was laughing at something he knew that I didn't know, and I was confused.

Jules suddenly appeared in the doorway. "Dinner is served, Dr. Hackman," he said.

We followed him into the dining room where we ate boiled beef and potatoes and buttered cabbage, topped off with wide wedges of warm lemon chess pie.

As Dr. Hackman leaned back from the table, unbuttoning the bottom button of his vest and lighting a cigar, Mother pulled back her chair and excused herself.

"Paul and I have had a long, tiring day," she said. "We should retire early."

Dr. Hackman suddenly leaned forward. "Please feel free to retire, Mrs. Karsten," he said. "We'll be hard at work early tomorrow morning. But would you mind leaving Paul with me for a little while? I think I should satisfy his curiosity."

I knew Mother was as puzzled as I was, but she quietly agreed and left the room.

Dr. Hackman put his cigar into a large, round holder and got up from the table. "Come with me, Paul," he said.

I followed him, wondering what would happen.

We went through the hallway in the opposite direction from the one I had taken earlier. We came to a door, which Dr. Hackman opened and propped with a small doorstop to keep it ajar. He reached for a string that turned on an electric light bulb, and I could see stairs going down to a dimly lit basement.

"This way," he said, as we carefully went down the stairs and entered a large room with a cement floor. I didn't pay attention to the pipes and barrels and all the things basements are usually filled with. Hardly able to breathe, I followed close behind Dr. Hackman to a screen that had been placed across a small alcove built into the wall at the far end of the room. What would be behind that screen? At that point I really didn't want to know!

Dr. Hackman removed the screen and stepped aside. I blinked, trying to adjust to the dim light, and then I saw it. I knew what it was. I had seen one like it in the museum, and it frightened me so much I never forgot it. There before me, inside the alcove, its glittering jeweled eyes seeming to stare right into mine, stood a tall, ornately painted Egyptian mummy!

4

The mummy!" Debbie interrupted. "That's what the men brought in that long box, wasn't it?"

"Yes," Mr. Karsten said. He spoke quietly, as though he remembered fearful things, while he continued the story:

I could only stare at it. Finally, I stammered, "Is — is it real?" I couldn't take my eyes off the mummy. Even in the dim light the painted face and shoulders seemed to shimmer as though the mummy was moving.

Dr. Hackman spoke sharply. "Of course it's real!" He paused, and placed a hand on the mummy. "It's the high point of my Egyptian collection! I can hardly believe my good fortune!"

I well remembered something my father had told me when we visited the museum and saw the mummies; so I asked Dr. Hackman, "How could you get a real mummy into this country, sir? My father told me that the Egyptian government doesn't allow anyone to take the mummies out of Egypt."

He winked at me. "Ah, ha! There are ways. It cost me a great deal to obtain this mummy." His beard waggled as he laughed. "Don't you agree with me it was well worth it?"

"The mummies I saw once in a museum had painted eyes," I told him. "This one has black jewels with gold around them."

"There were many Egyptian kings, or pharaohs," he explained. "Some were more important than others. Many of the tombs that have been discovered were vandalized by robbers who long ago stole the gold and jewels from them. But new tombs are uncovered all the time, some of them so secretly hidden over the years that their contents were left untouched. And I have been lucky!" He actually rubbed his hands together and grinned.

I looked more carefully at the mummy. There were small cracks in the painted material that covered the wrappings underneath, and at the bottom the wrappings had broken away. I could see the brown, knobby bones of some of the mummy's toes. I shuddered.

Dr. Hackman didn't seem interested in my answer. He was chuckling to himself, delighted with his possession. "Yes, it's well worth it," he said, "especially since I know how to protect myself from the pharaohs' curse."

"What curse?" I jumped backward, nearly falling.

He laughed and grabbed my arm to steady me. "Afraid, are you, Paul? Well, I assumed since you knew about the Egyptian government's ruling, that you would know the rest — that according to legend, anyone who disturbs one of the tombs or takes treasures from a tomb falls under the pharaohs' curse and is in danger of losing his life."

I took another step backward. "I — I don't I want to hear any more about mummies, sir."

He sighed. "Well, Paul, I am disappointed. I thought you would surely be interested in my collection of artifacts from Egyptian tombs."

My mouth fell open as I stared at him. He must have guessed what was in my mind, because he said, "No, this is the only mummy. I am talking about some alabaster jars, some small statues, and a few gold ornaments. I'm very proud of my collection."

"It sounds like something from a museum, sir," I said.

"Right you are!" His eyes glittered. "Some day this house will be my museum, and people will come from many lands to see my collection, and historians will come to study my writings. Oh, I'll be very famous! You'll see."

29

Something suddenly occurred to me. "Dr. Hackman, about that curse you mentioned — wouldn't that be on your jars and gold ornaments and statues, too?"

"Oh yes," he said, "but I told you the curse doesn't worry me. Nothing has happened. Well, not to me, at least." He looked at me sharply from the corners of his eyes and added, "Sooner or later you will probably hear from someone in town about an unfortunate accident that happened to a young man who had helped me bring some things from Egypt. He fell from the windows in your tower room. No matter what rumors you may hear, remember it was only an accident. Such a sorry, sorry situation."

But he didn't look sorry, and I didn't want to hear any more. I only wanted to get out of that basement! I mumbled something and kept edging toward the stairway. Dr. Hackman had turned back to the mummy and was examining it, when I said, "Will you please excuse me, sir?"

He nodded, so I turned and ran.

I raced all the way to Mother's room, again knocking loudly. She opened it so quickly I wondered if she had expected me to come.

She had tied a flowered wrapper over her nightgown and was holding a copy of *The Ladies' Home Journal*, one finger tucked between the pages, keeping her place.

"Dr. Hackman has an Egyptian mummy in his basement!" I blurted out. "It was in the crate that came with us from the train!" I shuddered again as I thought of being so close to that mummy and not even knowing it!

Mother put an arm around my shoulders and pulled me into the room, shutting the door quietly. She tossed the magazine to the floor and sat beside me on the bed.

As I told her what I had seen, she began to look puzzled, then distressed. When I finished, she asked, "Are you sure it was not just a plaster copy of a mummy?"

I shook my head. "Dr. Hackman will probably show it to you tomorrow. He's awfully proud of it."

She didn't answer, so I asked, "Isn't it against our country's laws to take something that belongs to another country?"

Mother sighed. "If so, no one does anything about it. When I began working with the history department at the university, I was amazed to find how many of the wealthy people in our country collect artifacts from other countries, even though it is against their laws to remove them. I'm afraid some of our large museums obtain items for their collections in the same way."

"Maybe that's why pharaohs put curses on their tombs," I said. "Maybe they thought that would stop people who wanted to take things."

"Oh, dear," Mother said. "I'm sure that Dr. Hackman was teasing you when he talked about a curse. We don't believe in superstitious things like that."

"He said he had protected himself against the curse, but he didn't tell me how." From the way he seemed to like secrets, I knew he probably never would tell me.

"I hope you realize there is nothing to be afraid of about Dr. Hackman's mummy or any silly tales about curses," Mother told me as she stood. "You should be pleased that he wants to share his interest with you."

I nodded. If I told Mother how I really felt, it would only make her worried and unhappy, so I kissed her good-night and went down the long hallway toward the door to my tower room.

When electric lights had been added to this house, no one had apparently thought of putting a light on that narrow, twisting stairway. The light from the hallway gave enough of a glow so that I could find my way along the lower two thirds of the stairway, but the upper stairs were dark, and I had to feel my way. I gripped the handrail and let the toes of my shoes explore the edges of the steps.

At last the door to my room was in front of me, and I opened it with trembling fingers. Once inside the room, I let out a long breath and leaned against the closed door.

Faintly, very faintly I heard someone else breathing, and I knew I wasn't alone. Someone else was in the room with me!

"Jules?" I whispered.

No one answered.

"Is someone here?"

Nothing. Not a sound.

I couldn't stand here all night, clutching the doorknob. And I couldn't run to my mother. My earlier fears had caused me to behave like a little child. No. I was twelve years old, and I had to grow up.

My eyes became adjusted to the dark. The curtainless windows let in enough of the thin moonlight so that I began to be able to make out the outlines of the furniture in my room. Across the room, next to the bed, was the lamp, and I slowly, carefully made my way toward it.

When I turned the switch and light burst through the room I was so relieved I could have shouted. The breathing I had heard had been only in my imagination. No one was here. But my eyes went to the wardrobe. It was large enough for someone to hide in. I ran to the wardrobe and threw open the doors. Nothing was inside but my few clothes.

I sat back on the bed, feeling both relieved and foolish. Suddenly I was so tired I could hardly keep my eyes open. As I pulled off my clothes and laid them neatly on the chair to wear tomorrow something dropped on the floor with a clink. The strange gold piece. I had forgotten all about it. Now I was too tired to think. I yawned and shivered, and dropped it into the top drawer of the chest. I'd try to remember to ask Dr. Hackman about it tomorrow.

The water in the pitcher was cold, as I knew it would be, but I poured it into the basin, took a small cloth and soap, and scrubbed myself until the water was gray and my body was clean. I pulled on my nightshirt and climbed into bed, turning off the light as I did so. I must have fallen asleep instantly.

Sometimes, when something wakes you from sleep, you don't know if you are asleep or awake; if what you heard had really happened or if it was just a part of your dream. So when I heard what sounded like a cry, it took a few minutes for me to wake up and try to figure out if I had heard it or only dreamed that I had heard it.

I lay perfectly still, listening to the silence. The cry wasn't repeated. Maybe it had been just a part of my dream. But it had seemed so real.

Had it been my mother?

No. There was no way I could have heard her

way up here in the tower. I tried to remember the cry. It had a strange sharpness to it, as though it had been made not by a human, but by an animal. And it was close enough so that it must have come from here, inside my room.

But I was alone, wasn't I?

I sat up in bed, my back pressed against the headboard, listening intently, trying to see. It didn't occur to me to turn on the lamp. The moonlight was bright now, and it was enough.

A rush of cool air made me shiver and pull the quilt to my chin. The windows! The one in the middle was open, its sash raised wide!

I knew good and well that I had not opened the window. I had been careful to stay away from those windows, remembering the cliff below and what Jules had said.

Maybe the window had blown open.

Ridiculous. The window had a sash that had to be raised. It couldn't blow open.

My instincts were to scoot down in bed and pull the covers over my head, but for some reason I couldn't understand I found myself climbing out of bed, my feet touching the cold wooden floor.

One slow step at a time I walked toward that open window.

5

P aul?"
       The voice punctured the odd, dreamlike
state I was in, and I whirled to see my mother
standing in the doorway.

"Good gracious," she said, hurrying toward the
window and pulling down the sash. "It's freezing
in this room! Too much night air could cause you
to become ill."

Wide awake now, with the night breeze blow-
ing through the room, I began to shiver. Mother
put an arm around my shoulders, leading me back
to my bed.

She tucked me in, fussing over me and patting
the quilt around my shoulders. Then she sat on the
edge of the bed and looked at me. "I'm sorry if
you're unhappy here." Her voice was soft and
carried so much grief she couldn't hide it. "I'm sure
you'll quickly get used to living here. When school
begins next month you'll meet other boys and girls
your age, and you'll have friends."

"I hope so," I murmured.

"Of course you will." She smiled and smoothed the hair from my forehead. "And I know I'll like my position here. It's going to take many years of work to get Dr. Hackman's papers and collections in order." She bent to kiss me.

"Get back to sleep now," she said. "I hope you feel better. No more bad dreams that will make you cry out again."

"Mother, I didn't cry out."

"But I thought I heard you. That's why I came."

I gulped and began to shiver again, even though my body heat was beginning to make the bed warm again. "Mother," I said, "this tower room is a long way from your room. If I had shouted at the top of my lungs, you couldn't have heard me." I added, "I heard a cry, too. That's what woke me."

She frowned. "I don't understand. Who would have made that cry?"

I suspected that the cry and the open window had something to do with the pharaohs' curse, but I couldn't tell my mother this.

"Maybe it was a night bird," I said. "We don't know the kinds of birds who live in this area. Remember the bird we heard once who sounded as though it was calling, 'Come here, come here,' and Father came in the room and said, 'Did you call me?' "

Mother laughed. "I remember. It was so funny!

And you're right. What we heard was probably a night bird."

She gave my shoulders one last pat and stood. "Sleep well, Paul. I'll see you in the morning." She quietly opened and closed the door to my room, and I could hear her soft footsteps descending the stairs. I hurried to the chest and scooped up the key to my bedroom door. Stumbling and fumbling, I managed to lock the door.

I was sure I'd never get back to sleep, so I was surprised to open my eyes and find my room filled with early sunlight. I dressed and made my way downstairs to the dining room, where Mother and Dr. Hackman were already finishing their breakfasts.

"Good morning," Mother said, smiling at me.

Dr. Hackman pulled a gold pocket watch from his vest pocket. "Nearly seven A.M. You've slept late, Paul."

"I'm sorry, sir." I pulled out a chair and climbed into it.

Dr. Hackman must have signaled Anna, because she appeared, her hands tucked under her apron again. "Paul will have his breakfast now, Anna," he said. He turned to me. "Paul, there is a job you could do for me this morning, if you'd be so kind."

"Of course, sir," I answered.

He smiled, but there was no friendliness in his

smile. It was as though he knew a joke I didn't know, a joke he was going to play on me, and I immediately mistrusted him.

"After you've eaten breakfast, Jules will give you a soft rag," he said. "I'd like you to polish the small metal statues you'll find in the parlor and the entry hall."

Those awful statues! The ones I had wanted to stay far away from! But I had no choice. "Yes, sir," I said.

Anna carried in a large plate of eggs and ham and buttered bread, and put it in front of me.

Dr. Hackman turned to Mother. "If you're ready, we can get to work now," he said. "I've had a desk and chair put into the room next to my office, and I'll show you where I'd like you to begin."

Mother pushed back her chair and patted my shoulder as she passed by. She walked with a little rustle and bounce. I knew she was eager to begin her new job.

But I wasn't eager to begin mine.

Anna stuck her head in the door and hissed, "Don't dawdle! He won't like it!" So I gulped down as much of the breakfast as I could manage and carried my plate to the kitchen.

Jules was there, bent almost double as he stacked wood in a box next to the stove. He looked up at me and straightened. "You're ready for your task, are you?" he said. "I'll find you a rag."

I waited until he handed it to me, then asked, "Who was crying in the house last night?"

Anna gave a little gasp, and Jules blinked. Other than that the expression on his face didn't change. "I didn't hear a cry," he said.

"I did. And Mother did, too. I told her it was probably a night bird, and that satisfied her. But I know it wasn't a night bird. I think it has to do with the accident that took place in the tower room. Please tell me what you know about it." I thought of the open window. "It may save my life."

Jules shook his head and said, "There is nothing we can tell you."

But Anna scowled. "We know very little. Whatever happened took place before we came to work here a few months ago."

"I thought you'd been here for years and years!"

"No." She looked at Jules. "Dr. Hackman has had trouble keeping servants."

"Why?"

Jules interrupted. "Probably because his house is so far from town. It's quiet and lonely here."

"It was one of the delivery people from town who told us what happened," Anna said. "Dr. Hackman's guest fell from the tower room. His body was sent back to Egypt."

"So he was Egyptian. Do you know anything else about him?" I thought of the gold piece. It must have belonged to him. "What happened to his belongings?"

She shrugged. "What I told you is all I know. If you want to learn more, you'll have to ask Dr. Hackman."

"I would advise against doing that," Jules said. He nervously glanced toward the door. "And I would advise against any more idle conversation like this. It's time that you got busy with your chore."

I began with the statues on the entry hall table. I hated them the most, so I wanted to get that part of the job over with. But I found, as I polished them, that they weren't as frightening as I had originally thought. They were made with great detail and beauty. The large one that I had disliked the most, a slender figure with a human body and a head like that of a deer, was so perfect it was almost real. Its slanted eyes were fringed with lashes and were opened wide as it stared straight ahead. But it didn't have horns, as a deer would have. It had long ears, like a mule's. It looked a great deal like the animal head that was scratched on the gold piece in my room.

As I rubbed it to a shine I accidentally twisted its base, and it came apart. There was a hollow place in the base, as though it were designed to hold something small. I was relieved that I hadn't broken the statue, and carefully fastened the base in place again.

I worked so hard that I was surprised when Jules came into the room and announced that it was one o'clock and dinner was served.

I hurried to wash my hands, finding again that I was the last one to come to the table.

"Are you enjoying your job?" Dr. Hackman asked me.

The mocking gleam in his eyes angered me. I sat up straight, looked directly into his eyes, and said, "I'm enjoying it very much, sir. I'm glad that you asked me to polish the statues. I've been able to see how beautiful they are."

"Oh," he said, and seemed surprised.

"But I have a question to ask, Dr. Hackman. Why does the tall statue have the head of an animal?"

Dr. Hackman shook out his napkin and laid it across his lap as Jules carried in a huge tureen of soup and placed it in front of him. "I believe you are referring to the statue of Anubis. He has the head of a jackal."

"What's a jackal?"

"It's a type of wild dog that hunts at night." Dr. Hackman ladeled out bowls of soup and passed them to Mother and to me. "It has a sharp bark, almost like a cry, and lives in countries in Asia and Africa."

The soup was too hot, and I waited for it to cool. "I still don't understand, sir," I said. "Even if jackals live in Egypt, is there a reason for the statue to have a jackal head? And what does the name, Anubis, mean?"

Dr. Hackman put down his spoon, patted his lips and beard with his napkin, and leaned toward me. "Why, Paul, the god Anubis, who had the body of a man and the head of a jackal, is the guardian of the tombs. It was he who watched over the dead who were preserved as mummies and he who made sure that no one would disturb their final resting places."

He grinned, and I was sure that he knew he had frightened me again. "Anubis is the one to watch out for, Paul. It is he who carries out the pharaohs' curse!"

6

Jeff gasped. "Are you saying that Anubis made that cry in the night?"

"Don't mind Jeff," Debbie said. Her eyes were wide. "Please just go on with the story!"

Mr. Karsten paused a moment, then said:

Mother seemed embarrassed. I could tell that she didn't want to reproach her employer, but she felt she must protect me. "Paul has an active imagination," she said. "Perhaps it would be better not to dwell on some of the legends."

Dr. Hackman nodded toward Mother. "As you wish," he said.

Jules took away the soup plates and brought the next course: some kind of fish baked in a thick sauce and surrounded by overcooked squash and potatoes. Our plates were heaped high, and I tried to choke down as much of the food as possible. I didn't have much appetite.

Dr. Hackman ignored me and began talking to

Mother about the mummy. Apparently he had shown it to her, and she seemed quite interested, asking him lots of questions about pyramids and their construction and the Valley of the Kings, where many of the tombs had been found.

But when Jules came to clear away the plates, Mother said, "I don't believe Paul will have dessert, since he did not eat his vegetables."

"Then may I please be excused?" I asked. I was eager to get outside and run down the open expanse of hillside. I wanted to explore the woods that surrounded our clearing. And I thought, if it wasn't too far, I would like to walk into town. I had had only a glimpse of it as we drove from the railway depot.

"You may," Mother said. "Exercise would be good for you. Go outside instead of cooping yourself up with one of your dime novels."

"Yes, ma'am," I said. In the bottom drawer of the chest in my room was a copy of *Tip Top Weekly* with a new Frank Merriwell story in it. I was eager to read it, but for now I just wanted to get away from this house.

"Before you go outside, Paul," Dr. Hackman said, "there is something you could do for me. You will find a box against the wall next to the door to the basement. Will you please take it down to the basement?"

"Yes, sir," I answered. I didn't like the idea of

going into that basement again, but I wouldn't look in the direction of the mummy. I planned to put the box down quickly and rush back up the stairs.

"Thank you, Paul," he said. "Just put the box next to the alcove the mummy is in."

He turned to talk to Mother, but I hadn't missed his quick, gleeful look. He knew how I felt about that mummy. Was trying to frighten me a game with him? I tucked my chair back under the table and left the room.

I was so eager to get this terrible chore over with that I ran down the hallway, threw open the door to the basement, and turned on the light. The box on the floor wasn't heavy. I had no idea what was in it, and I didn't care. I quickly descended the stairs. However, at the foot of the stairs I paused. It was going to take all the courage I had to walk over to that mummy.

I made my way across the basement, moving step by step toward the alcove. The room was so cold I shivered. I imagined I could hear small rustlings, tiny creaks of the house itself, even the sound of shallow breathing.

I kept telling myself that it was my own breath I heard. I wouldn't allow myself to panic. I resolved to not look at the mummy. If I didn't look at it, I could even pretend it wasn't there. But I couldn't help myself. I had to look.

As I came close to the painted figure that rested

upright against the wall, something disturbed me. There was something wrong, something different about the mummy.

The golden, jeweled eyes were gone, leaving blank, gray sockets that looked like gaping sores in the painted decorations! Without his golden eyes that covered the sightless sockets in his skull, the mummy was even more terrifying!

As I stared at the mummy I heard a sound that I knew wasn't my imagination. It was only a faint sound, but I had heard it before. It was sharp and it was sorrowful, like a faraway cry.

Had it come from the mummy? Had it come from behind me? I couldn't tell. I dropped the box at the mummy's feet and ran, scrambling and tripping, across the room and up the stairs, grabbing at the doorknob.

But the door was locked!

I pounded on the door and yelled and screamed. I thought I could feel something coming up the steps behind me.

When the door finally was opened, I threw myself into the hallway and into Jules, causing him to stagger backward.

"Someone locked the door!" I shouted.

"No one locked the door," Jules said. He pointed to the doorstop, which was at the edge of the top step. "You should have propped the door to keep it ajar." He calmly reached in and pulled the string that turned off the electric light bulb, adding, "When you came to the basement with Dr. Hackman, didn't he use the doorstop?"

I nodded, too embarrassed to answer. Of course I remembered. I'd been so terrified of having to go into the basement, I hadn't thought of what I was doing.

"I have to tell Dr. Hackman something!" I said.

"He's working and should not be disturbed," Jules said.

"This is important!" I shouted it over my shoulder, because I was already down the hallway toward Dr. Hackman's office.

The door was open, and I burst through. Dr. Hackman looked up from his papers, surprised. He was wearing that odd yachting cap again, and for an instant I wondered what good luck he was hoping for now.

"Dr. Hackman!" I blurted out. "The mummy's golden eyes are gone!"

I suppose I expected Dr. Hackman to be as concerned as I was. Instead, he just smiled and said, "Of course they are. Please don't over-excite yourself, Paul."

"But I thought — "

He waved a pudgy hand in the air as though it didn't matter what I thought. "The gold and the jewels that decorated the eyes are quite valuable in themselves, and we have little protection here from thieves, so I have hidden them," he said. He giggled. "Only I know the secret."

"Oh," I said. "I'm sorry to have bothered you, sir."

"Did you leave the box in the basement?"

"Yes, sir."

His eyes twinkled again in that wicked way as he asked, "And did you remember to prop open the door before you entered, so you wouldn't be locked in the basement?"

He knew I wouldn't remember. At least, I was sure he hoped I wouldn't remember. I tried not to show what I was feeling and asked, "May I please be excused, sir? I'd like to go for a walk."

"Of course," he said, and bent over his papers, a satisfied smile still on his face.

"Is that all he told you — that he knew the secret?" Debbie asked. "Didn't he give you any clues?"

"Obviously, he didn't want me to know where the golden eyes were hidden."

Debbie sighed. "I just thought he might have said something that would help."

"Help?" Mr. Karsten asked.

Jeff glared at Debbie. "Be quiet," he said.

Debbie looked guilty and quickly said, "I didn't mean to interrupt. Please go on with the story."

"Ask questions. I don't mind," Mr. Karsten said.

He leaned back in his chair and began to speak:

I put on my cap but left my jacket. The air was warm and honey-sweet with the fragrance of clover and pollen and bees. I didn't take the driveway from the house, but instead strode through the ankle-high grasses on the hill and through the trees until I found the main road. I walked along the road, the sun warm on my back, hoping I would find someone to talk to so I could forget all about Dr. Hackman and his horrible mummy.

Unfortunately, I seemed to be all alone in the world, and the town must have been in the opposite direction. I passed a couple of farms, but the houses were far from the road; and the people who lived in them were not in sight.

The sun was low in the sky by the time I turned to walk back. I took the same route returning, so that I cut through the trees and came out in the clearing at the bottom of the hill. The sky was on fire in the west, and that same fire was captured by the front windows of the house, so that it glowed as though the sunset had been captured inside. I hurried up the hill and into the house. I had plenty of time to wash in the basin in my room and read the first part of *Frank Merriwell's Great Victory, or the Effort of His Life* before I heard the bell announcing supper.

The meal was pleasant, and my walk had made

me hungry; so I cleaned my plate, and Mother beamed at me in approval.

Dr. Hackman was in a jovial mood. "We have worked hard today," he said. "Perhaps this evening you would like to join me in the parlor. I have some records we can play on the gramophone, and some fine stereopticon slides to look at."

"Thank you," Mother said. "We'd enjoy that."

Mother might, but I didn't. I hated the idea of having to spend every evening in the parlor with Dr. Hackman. I wished Mother and I were somewhere else. Anywhere else but in this awful place with terrible Dr. Hackman; so I was glad when Mother finally announced it was time for us to retire. I went up to my room and this time locked the door.

I made very sure that the windows were not only shut, but locked, before I crawled under my quilt. The long walk had been good for me. It had cleared the fear from my mind. I must have fallen asleep as soon as I touched the pillow.

When I awoke the moon was high in the sky, and the room was lit with moonlight. Something had awakened me. Something had alerted me. I sat up in bed, wondering what it had been, until I heard the slow footsteps coming up the stairway to my tower room.

I crept to the door, making sure this time the key was in the keyhole and the door was locked.

The footsteps were coming closer. Someone was trying to be quiet and very careful, but occasionally a board in the stairs would creak or snap.

"Mother?" I called in a low voice.

The footsteps stopped. If it had been my mother she would have answered me.

"Who's there?" I asked, and my voice was so loud in the room that I jumped, startled.

I waited for what seemed to be a very long time. I didn't move. I just listened.

Finally, the footsteps began again. I tiptoed across my room and picked up the little desk chair. As quietly as I could manage, I wedged it against the door, tucking it under the doorknob. It was another barrier to whoever was on the stairs outside my room.

A board shifted, and I felt it move. Someone had reached the top of the stairs and was standing on the other side of the door.

I could hardly breathe. I didn't know what to do. If I called out, would anyone hear me? Would anyone come?

A faint scratching began on the other side of my door, the kind of a scratching an animal might make.

Terrified, unable to think, I whispered, "What do you want?"

And a voice whispered back, "Where are my eyes?"

7

I felt as though someone had dumped a bucket of cold water over me, and I had turned to a block of ice. I couldn't move. I heard the whisper again, "Where are my eyes?"

Strangely enough, it wasn't the golden, jeweled eyes of the mummy that came to my mind. It was the pair of eyes scratched into the small gold coin that lay in the top drawer of the chest in my room. I could see the design as clearly as though I'd been shown a photograph.

I thought of the man who had fallen from the window in this room. Had something been after the coin while he had it in his possession? Is that why something came to him and why it had come to me?

The scratching became more insistent, and the doorknob rattled. The key shook, and I was afraid it would fall from the lock. If it was on the floor, near the door, maybe whoever was out there could reach it! With clammy fingers I pulled the key from the lock, gripping it tightly.

Instantly the scratching stopped, and there was a snuffling sound at the keyhole, as though an animal were sniffing there.

I was trapped in this room. There was no way I could get out. Desperately I thought of one thing I could do. I ran to the chest, yanked the top drawer open and pulled out the coin.

As I did so, a sharp, barking cry came from the other side of the door. I unlocked the sash of the middle window, and tugged it open. I felt as though a wind was trying to push me out, but I held the window frame tightly, leaned over the sill, and dropped the coin. I heard a soft clink as it hit the ground below.

I pushed myself back, dropping to the floor, and sat against the wall panting for breath.

Suddenly it occurred to me that all sensations of wind and whispers were gone, that nothing was on the stairs outside my room, that whatever had been here had left as the coin had fallen. I got to my knees and peered over the windowsill. The moon was full and bright, so I was able to see everything. All was silent. Nothing moved. Not even a light breeze ruffled the tree branches. Something gleamed on a rock below the window. What else could it be but the coin?

Now that my fear had gone, I began to grow angry. All this horror was because of Dr. Hackman. I understood what he meant when he said he had protected himself against the pharaohs' curse. He knew that strange coin had the power to draw the evil toward whoever possessed it, so that evil would be drawn away from him.

I looked again at the tiny, gleaming object below, and another thought occurred to me.

What if Dr. Hackman found the coin? I had no way of knowing if he could sense the location of the coin. There were so many strange things about the man. If he found it would he put it back in my room? I didn't think so, because he'd know I would search for it.

What if he put it in Mother's room?

I groaned. I couldn't let anything like this happen to Mother! She was so trusting of Dr. Hackman that she wouldn't be able to protect herself.

I had to retrieve the coin and hide it in a place where it wouldn't be found.

As fast as I could I dressed, not allowing myself to think about what I was doing, so that I couldn't change my mind.

Holding my breath, I unlocked the door to my room and inched it open. The stairs were dark, and I could see nothing. But I gripped the handrail and slowly crept down the steps. I suppose at any second I expected something to jump up and grab me, and it was awfully hard to breathe.

Finally I was in the long hallway of the second floor. Moonlight came through the windows opposite the wide stairway to the ground floor, so it was easier for me to see where I was going. I paused outside Mother's door and listened intently, but I could hear nothing.

When I reached the entry hall I stopped and looked carefully down each side of the main hallway. A door was open at the far end of the hall on my right, spilling a bright puddle of light into that part of the hallway. I recognized the door as the one leading to the basement, and for a moment I was so frightened I wanted to race upstairs and lock myself in my room and not come out until daylight.

But I knew what I had to do.

Quietly I opened the front door and went outside. The night air was cold, and I wished I had thought to bring my jacket. I walked across the grass, my socks getting wet from the dew, and rounded the house.

It would have helped if I had made this trip during daylight hours. The moonlight created deep, deceptive shadows, and occasionally I stumbled. There was no fence, nothing to protect me from the cliff's edge. I hugged the side of the house, climbing over large boulders, until I found myself under the tower that was my room.

Ahead of me, resting on a smooth boulder, was the triangular gold piece. But close on my right side was a sheer drop to the valley, and I knew I couldn't slip. There would be no second chance. Far below me there seemed to be steps cut into the rock. I couldn't imagine how one would get to them or why they were there. But at the moment I had more important things on my mind.

On my hands and knees I crept slowly toward the coin.

I stopped once as I thought I heard breathing behind me. I looked back, but the shadows were long and dark, and I could see nothing that moved.

Just a few inches more, and my fingers closed around the coin.

I worked my way backward, inch by inch, my toes hunting for solid places, until finally I had reached ground where I could stand and turn around. The moon was lower in the sky, and it had become darker, but I used the walls of the house as my guide, until I was back on the lawn in front of the house.

It was hard to walk up those porch steps and enter the house again. Now that the coin was in my possession again, whatever horrors roamed through the house might be after me! What was I going to do with the coin? Where could I hide it?

I quietly shut the large door, and stood with my back to it, facing the entry hall. Before me the weird statues gleamed in the moonlight.

The statues! I clapped one hand over my mouth as I gave a loud sigh of relief. I remembered the hollow base on the statue of Anubis. Surely the coin would fit inside, and Dr. Hackman would never think of looking for it there, especially since he suspected I was afraid of that statue.

I picked up the statue, pried off the base, popped the coin inside, and wedged the base back into place.

The statue began to grow warm in my hand, and I dropped it on the table, jumping back.

As I watched, it began to tremble and glow!

I didn't wait to see any more. I scrambled up the stairs as fast as I could, and pounded on the door to Mother's room until she opened it.

"Oh dear," she said. "Not another nightmare, Paul?" Her eyelids heavy with sleep and her hair tousled, she bent to put her arms around me, but I twisted from her grasp and locked the door.

Mother stepped back as I dragged the purple armchair to the door and wedged it under the lock.

"Paul!" she gasped, "what's the matter with you? What are you doing?"

She moved toward the lamp near her bed, but I said, "Don't turn on the light, Mother! Just sit down, please, and listen to me!"

Mother sat on the edge of the bed, and I held her hand.

"You're trembling," she began, but I interrupted.

"Don't talk. Let me tell you what is happening in this house."

My words tumbled out as I told her everything from the beginning. When I ended with the description of how the statue of Anubis was moving and glowing, my practical mother shook her head in disbelief. "Paul, that couldn't be. Don't you see, dear? You had a nightmare that seemed very real to you. I'll put on my wrapper, and we'll go downstairs so that I can prove to you that you dreamed it."

"No!" I tried not to shout. "We can't go downstairs! We'll have to stay here until morning. Then we can leave this house!"

"But, Paul — "

A wild, terrified scream that came from somewhere on the ground floor interrupted whatever Mother was going to say.

8

We could only stare at each other. Our hands were gripped together so tightly my fingers hurt, and we couldn't move.

Again there was a scream, but it was farther away. And we heard a thumping, banging sound.

"I think that came from the direction of the basement," I whispered.

Mother shook her head and got to her feet. "Paul, someone is in trouble. We've got to help."

"What can we do?" I tugged at her hands, unwilling to let her open the bedroom door.

Mother was becoming her practical self again. "For one thing, we can call the police."

"But we'd have to go downstairs and into Dr. Hackman's office."

"That's right. Now, if you'll let go of my hands, Paul, I'll put on my wrapper."

"Whatever is down there might come after us!"

"Nonsense." Mother was busy tying her wrapper and aiming her toes into her slippers. "It sounded to me as though someone might have fallen down stairs. Maybe it was Jules. Maybe Dr. Hackman. Whoever it was needs help."

As I followed Mother into the hallway I almost shouted with relief. A gray, early-morning light filtered through the large windows over the stairway, and by the time we arrived downstairs we were easily able to see.

I glanced quickly at the table. The statue of Anubis still rested there! I wondered if the coin was still inside the base. I was eager to know, but not brave enough to try to find out!

The basement door was closed, but Mother opened it, reached in, and pulled the string that turned on the light. "Dr. Hackman?" she called.

No one answered, and we could see no sign of disturbance at this end of the basement room.

With Mother I searched the downstairs rooms. All looked as it should.

Anna joined us in the hallway, Jules behind her. She was also in a wrapper, with her hair loose around her shoulders, but Jules had dressed.

"We heard it, too," she said to Mother.

"Will you please wake Dr. Hackman?" Mother asked Jules.

We waited quite a while until he came back, shaking his head. "There is no sign of Dr. Hackman," he told us.

"Then I will call the police," Mother said. And she did.

Mr. Karsten leaned back in his chair and said, "So that's the story of Hackman's Hill. The police came and searched for Dr. Hackman, but there was no sign of him."

"It was that coin, wasn't it?" Debbie said. "When you gave it back to Anubis by putting it into his statue it must have given him some kind of power."

"There has to be a logical explanation," Jeff said. "I don't believe in powers and superstitions and Egyptian curses. I think Dr. Hackman was just mean enough to have fun scaring a little kid."

"But Dr. Hackman disappeared," Debbie said.

"And so did his mummy," Mr. Karsten said. "As I told Jeff last year, the director of a museum in Egypt posted a reward of ten thousand dollars for anyone who could find the mummy."

"Did you look for it?"

"Not I," Mr. Karsten said. "Jules and Anna, Mother and I left the house that very day. Even though Mother got a job with a firm here in town, I vowed never to go near Hackman's Hill again."

"Didn't you want the reward?"

"Not that much. A few people tried for it. A pair of treasure hunters thought they could find the golden eyes, but they could not stay in the house a single night. Someone saw them drive from town as though they were being chased. And a "ghosthunter," who had written books about ghost lights and shapes he had seen, came to the house. But soon after midnight he ran screaming from the house and refused to tell anyone what caused him to shake like a small tree in the wind. The house stands just as it had been. It has never even been robbed or vandalized. The people who lived in these parts were so terrified of the house that they refused to go near it; so soon the house was almost forgotten. The money for the reward is still held by the bank. The reward is still unclaimed."

"I'd like to get that reward," Jeff murmured.

Mr. Karsten's eyebrows drew down in a frown. "I told you the story, because I thought it would entertain you. I would never have told you about the reward if I had imagined you'd go into that house," he said. "I strongly caution you against it."

Jeff didn't answer. He glanced at Debbie. She barely nodded, a signal only he could see. Golden eyes? Strange cries in the night? Scary things that climbed stairs in the dark? Maybe Mr. Karsten thought they were still in the old Hackman house, but Jeff didn't. He didn't believe in curses and all that stuff, and he wasn't going to let them frighten him or keep him from his search. He was glad that Debbie was with him all the way in this adventure. That ten-thousand-dollar reward for finding the missing mummy was going to be theirs!

PART TWO:
THE HORROR

9

As Jeff and Debbie left Mr. Karsten's house, Jeff pulled his coat collar around his ears. The wind had grown much colder. They scurried across the street and reached the shelter of Grandpa's porch before either of them spoke.

"Do you believe everything happened just the way Mr. Karsten said it did in his story?" Debbie asked.

"I already told you what I thought — that Dr. Hackman was just being mean and having fun scaring a little kid."

"But why would Dr. Hackman disappear? And the mummy, too?"

"I don't know. Maybe Mr. Karsten was just building the story up to make it really scary. And maybe the grown-ups didn't tell him everything. Remember, he was only around ten years old."

Debbie stamped the snow from her boots. "But he'd be old enough to see what was going on."

"Are you backing out?" Jeff asked. "Are you

saying you don't want to go with me?"

"I'm going," Debbie said. "Hey, we do things together. Right?" She paused. "But be honest, Jeff. Won't you feel creepy in that house after what Mr. Karsten told us?"

Jeff nodded. "I guess. But all the things he told us about happened at night, not in the daytime. We'll just do our searching for the mummy in the daylight."

"When do you want to go to the Hackman house?"

"How about right now? We'll have to bring flashlights and batteries."

"And lots of film packs."

"And I'd better take my pocket knife and borrow one of Grandpa's screwdrivers."

"Oh! I can't forget my camera! I may get a winning picture for the contest."

Jeff grinned. "You bet. A picture of a mummy!"

"I'll make some sandwiches to take with us," Debbie said. "We may need something to eat."

Jeff shook his head. "What a time to think of food!"

The door opened, and Grandpa poked his head out. "I thought I heard voices," he said, "but I couldn't imagine your staying out here in the cold when you could be inside where it's warm."

They hurried into the house, pulling off their coats and scarves.

"I hope that storm misses us." Grandma looked up from her chair by the fireplace. "We've had one of the worst spells of weather for March that I can remember."

While Jeff had been packing for this trip to his grandparents, his mother had tucked a flashlight and extra batteries into his suitcase over his protests.

"So if you have to get up in the night you can find the bathroom down the hall," she had said.

"Mom, that's crazy!"

"No, it isn't. I know from experience. There are lots of little tables and what-nots in that hall, and you could break a toe."

He had grumbled at the time, but now he was glad the flashlight were there.

He'd have to get a flashlight for Debbie. There was a big one in the kitchen, and Grandma would probably let them borrow it without asking questions. In one of the kitchen drawers he had seen a sturdy-looking screwdriver. He didn't think they'd mind if he borrowed it. Screwdrivers were handy for all sorts of things.

Jeff got the flashlight and batteries from his room. When he got downstairs, Debbie was in the kitchen, stuffing sandwiches around the camera and film in her camera bag.

Jeff held out the extra batteries. "Can you fit these in your case?"

"Sure," she said, taking them. "Grandma came in to see what I was doing, and I asked if we could borrow her flashlight when we took our walk. She said yes and went back to the living room to watch her favorite soap opera."

"Where's Grandpa?"

"He went to town. Grandma said he was arranging a surprise for us." She gave a satisfied sigh. "Well, everything's ready."

Jeff grinned. "Is there anything you haven't thought of?"

"Cookies," she said. "Thanks for reminding me." The camera bag was full, so she put on her coat, grabbed handsful of cookies from the cookie jar, and stuffed them into her pockets.

Debbie was already dressed to go outside. "Come on," she said. "If we're going to go mummy hunting, let's get started."

Jeff grabbed the screwdriver from the drawer and stuffed it into his deep coat pocket with the flashlight; put on his boots, scarf, cap, mittens, and coat; and followed Debbie out the back door.

The snow on the road was well packed, so walking was easy. It was the cold wind that made the going difficult. They trudged along in silence until they came to the place in the road where the day before they had cut into the woods and found the clearing.

"Are you sure this is the right place?" Debbie asked.

"There are our footprints." Jeff led the way, and in just a short while they had stepped through the edge of the forest and were standing near the foot of Hackman's Hill.

In the gray light of morning, the house looked more gloomy and in worse repair than before. This time Jeff didn't feel that someone in the house was watching him. The dilapidated building seemed empty and totally deserted.

Puffing and grunting they made it up the hill. Debbie moved toward the porch, but Jeff held out a hand. "Some of the boards are rotten. Be careful," he said. Gingerly he picked his way to the front door. The knob wouldn't turn, no matter how he tugged at it. It hadn't occurred to him that the massive door would be locked. He should have thought of that.

Debbie followed him. "What's the matter?"

"The door's locked," he said.

With one mitten-covered hand Debbie reached out, turned the knob, and opened the door. "No it isn't," she said. "You must have turned the knob the wrong way."

He joined her at the front door, which now stood wide open. "Who pulled the door open like that?" he asked.

She shrugged. "The wind, probably."

They looked at each other. "Well, let's go inside," Jeff finally said. "We can't just stand out here."

Debbie shut the front door behind them, as Jeff studied the entry hall. It was still just as Mr. Karsten had described it, although the drapes that covered the windows were tattered, and part of the carved railing on the stairway was broken. Everything was covered with a thick layer of dust, and cobwebs clung to the walls and windows and to the small statues on the round table in the center of the room.

"It's there!" Debbie pointed to a metal statue with a human body and the head of a jackal, which rested on the center of the table. The statue was facing them.

Jeff took a step backward. Suddenly he wanted to leave this house. He would have turned and run, dragging Debbie with him, but he remembered the reward. He had to win that reward.

Debbie put her flashlight and camera case on a nearby chair. She pulled out her camera and aimed it at the statue. The bright flash and the whirring sound, as she took the picture, were so jarring and out of place that Jeff winced.

Neither of them spoke as she waited for the picture to take shape. But in the distance, along the hall to the right, there was the distinct sound of a door being shut.

Jeff's voice was raspy as he managed to say, "Must have been the wind again."

"Sure," Debbie said, but she moved closer to Jeff and added, "I can see why no one ever came into this house to rob it. This place is so creepy I feel like someone's watching us."

"Cut it out, Debbie," Jeff said. "We've got to decide where to start our search."

Debbie clutched his arm. "Jeff!" she whispered. "Look at the picture!"

Her hand was shaking so hard that Jeff couldn't see. "What's wrong with the picture?" he asked.

"Anubis!" she said. "All the other statues are in the picture, but not his! Anubis didn't show up!"

10

Jeff grabbed her hand and studied the print. "How can you tell what's in your picture and what isn't? It's blurred because you moved the camera."

"My hand was shaking. That's why it's blurred. But that doesn't matter. Look! His statue is taller than the others. Shouldn't there be something in the picture that stands up higher than everything around it?"

"Calm down," Jeff said. "Why don't you just take another picture? You need an awful lot of practice, if you're going to win a contest."

"Never mind. I'll take one later. I don't like the way that statue is looking at me."

"Don't be dumb," Jeff said. "Statues can't look at people." He hoped Debbie wouldn't notice that the statue made him nervous, too.

"Where shall we start our search?" Debbie asked.

"I suppose in Dr. Hackman's office. From what

Mr. Karsten told us, it's along this hallway to our left."

"You can't think you'll find the mummy in there!"

Jeff groaned. "Of course not. I'm going to look through his papers. Maybe there's a clue written somewhere."

Before they entered the hallway, Debbie pointed to the archway overhead. "There's the carving Mr. Karsten told us about. 'ONLY I KNOW THE SECRET.' It should say secrets, because Dr. Hackman must have had a lot of secrets."

"The biggest secret is what happened to his mummy."

"No," Debbie said. "The biggest secret is what happened to him."

They looked into a number of rooms, each with a key still in its lock, until they found the office.

"It's a mess," Debbie said. "But I'll take a picture of it before you go in there." The camera flashed.

Jeff looked at the pile of papers and books on the desk and on the floor, and groaned. There was no way he could read through all that stuff.

"I think this picture is turning out all right," Debbie said. "You can go in now."

Jeff brushed some cobwebs off the desk chair and sat in it. He pulled off his gloves. Then he picked up a sheet of paper on top of one of the piles and shook off a dead spider. "This is just a letter from a book publisher." He threw it down and pulled open a drawer. "Anything written about a mummy wouldn't be out in the open. It's hidden somewhere."

"I bet the police went through those drawers," Debbie said. "You won't find anything in there that would help."

Jeff poked through one of the drawers anyway. Papers, just more piles of papers. He leaned back and said, "I saw a real old movie on TV. This guy had a library, and he hid his wife's jewelry in a fake book on one of the shelves. Maybe that's where Dr. Hackman hid the mummy's golden eyes. Maybe there's something there that will tell where the mummy is, too."

"Good idea!" Debbie said. "I'll even help you look, only let me take a picture of the library first."

Jeff jumped out of the chair and ran past Debbie into the hallway. He was excited now that he had a direction to follow. "The library is right next door!"

Impatiently, he waited for Debbie to take her picture, then hurried into the room, studying the bookshelves on all four walls. "They all look the same. Cupboards on the bottom, then books all the way to the ceiling. I'll take this wall, and you take the one with the window in it. Just pull out every book and examine it, in case it's hollowed out, and be sure to look behind it."

Jeff began to work, tugging at the dusty books on the bottom shelf. He was so intent on what he might find that he wasn't paying attention to Debbie, and she had to repeat what she had said.

"Jeff! Aren't you listening? I told you to come here to the window! Now!"

He climbed to his feet and joined her at the window that looked over the wide clearing in front of the house. "What do you want me to see?" he asked.

She clutched his arm. "What *can* you see?"

The clearing and woods were hidden by strong gusts of snow that swirled around the house.

"It's the storm!" Debbie whispered.

"I didn't think it would get here so soon," Jeff said.

"Maybe we'd better go back to Grandpa's house now," Debbie said. She sounded as though she wanted to cry.

Jeff's stomach hurt as he stared at the blinding mass of snow. "We can't, Debbie. It's too far, and we couldn't see where we were going. We'd just get lost."

"They'll worry about us! What will they do?"

"They may call the constable's office. I know they won't try to go out to look for us, because they couldn't."

Jeff and Debbie watched the snow for a few more

minutes. Finally Debbie said, "Jeff, we can't leave this house, can we?"

He shook his head.

She shivered. "That means we might be here after dark."

"Hey," Jeff said, trying to sound brave and knowing he didn't make it. "We've got flashlights and extra batteries. No problem. Anyhow, the storm might be over soon, and we can leave."

"Promise? As soon as it's over?"

Jeff thought about the reward; but right now, feeling trapped, he was as eager to get out of this place as Debbie was.

"Promise," he said. "Since we can't go anywhere, why don't we get back to work?"

Jeff went to the shelf and picked up the next book. "*Secrets of the Lost Tribes*," he read aloud. "This guy Hackman was really big on secrets."

He shook the book, checked the shelf behind it, and put it back. He was reaching for the next book when he heard what sounded like a muffled cry.

"Hey, Debbie," he said, turning toward her. "Don't come apart. We'll get back to Grandpa's all right."

Debbie stared at him. "What are you talking about?"

"Weren't you crying?"

"Of course not." Her eyes opened wider as she added, "I thought that sound came from you!"

78

Jeff scrambled to his feet. He was so scared, he was afraid his teeth would rattle together if he tried to speak.

Debbie grabbed him around the neck and hung on so tightly that he nearly strangled before he was able to pry loose her arms.

"Don't do that! I've got to breathe!" he yelled.

"Something's in the house with us!" she answered. She lunged at him again, but he sidestepped her.

"Wait a minute. We can't do anything if you're going to keep jumping me like that."

Debbie backed up against the shelves. "What was that noise?" she whispered.

"Probably the wind."

"Sure it was the wind. The wind that opens and shuts doors and makes that awful crying sound. You've got to think up a better answer than that!"

"I honestly don't know what it was. I really wasn't paying much attention. It might have even been a bird."

"That's what Mr. Karsten told his mother, you jerk face! Birds don't go out in blizzards!"

"Hey, let's not get mad at each other. That won't help."

Debbie slid down and sat on the floor. "I know, Jeff. I'm sorry. I'm just so scared."

Jeff tried to convince himself as much as Debbie. "Old houses make a lot of noise. I know, because we used to live in one. They're always popping and creaking. That's probably the noise we heard."

"You really think so?"

"Sure."

There was silence as they listened for a few moments, both of them wondering what they'd do if they'd hear the sound again. Finally Jeff said, "Well, I don't know about you but, since we're stuck here for a while, I'm going to get back to these books."

"Okay," Debbie said. She scrambled to her feet and went to the window wall.

Jeff soon became intent upon the books. Some of them looked like the kind only scholars could plow through, but some looked interesting enough to read. One he opened was filled with photographs, and a picture of an ornate mummy caught his attention.

"Debbie," he said. "Come here and look at this! Here's a really great-looking mummy."

He raised his head. "Debbie?"

Debbie wasn't there.

Jeff jumped up so fast he banged his knee on the shelf. Hopping on one foot, trying to rub his knee, he called, "Debbie, where are you?"

He ran to the door to the hallway. "Debbie!" he shouted. "Debbie!"

But Debbie didn't answer.

11

Jeff ran down the hallway, shouting, "Debbie, where are you?" He turned and ran back, not knowing which direction to take. "I can't panic," he said aloud, and he made himself stop and think.

That's when he heard the thumping.

It wasn't very loud, and it seemed to come from the library. Carefully, quietly, he went to the door of the library and waited, listening for the sound again.

Another thump. But it wasn't from the library. It seemed to come from inside the wall in the next room. That wall was on the outside of the house. Was it just a tree branch hitting the house in the wind?

Jeff slumped against the door frame. He hadn't wanted Debbie to come here, but she had, and he felt responsible for her. After all, it had been his idea to search the old Hackman house. What would he do if he couldn't find her?

"Wait till you see what I discovered!" Debbie shouted from behind him.

Jeff jumped straight up in the air. "What do you think you're doing, scaring me like that?"

"Oh," Debbie said. "I didn't mean to scare you. I was just doing some investigating."

"Where? You didn't answer when I yelled for you."

"I couldn't. It was dusty and dirty in there, and I was afraid I'd get a spider in my mouth."

For the first time he noticed the smudges on her face. He helped her brush cobwebs and dust from the shoulders of her coat. "In where?" he asked.

"C'mere," she said, pulling him into the library. "See that cupboard on the end? Well, I got tired of just checking out the books, so I began looking in the cupboards below the shelves. The one at this end had an open space. I think a panel must have been there at one time. Anyhow, I could see something beyond it, and it had a tiny window in it. I crawled into it, stood up, and found myself in a passageway. It wasn't very long, so I followed it and walked into a closet in Dr. Hackman's office, and out of the office and came and told you about it."

"Why didn't you tell me before you crawled in there?"

"Maybe I should have," Debbie said. "I don't know. I just found myself there before I thought much about it. Do you want to see it?"

"I wonder."

"Wonder what?"

"If there are other passageways in this house."

They looked at each other. "The mummy!" they said, almost at the same time.

Debbie gasped. "What if the mummy had been in that passageway? What if I'd crawled right into it? Oh, no! I would have died, and you would have had to drag my body out of there!"

"I wouldn't have found your body," Jeff said. "I wouldn't have known where you were. You can't do that again. We have to stick together!"

Debbie nodded. "Right. Should we forget the books and go looking for passageways?"

Jeff sat on the floor. "Yeah. But first of all, let's think this out. We can't just run around banging on walls and opening closets."

Debbie sat beside him. He reached over and pulled a trailing spiderweb from her hair. "Are you sure the passageway you were in just went between two rooms?" Jeff asked.

"I'm positive."

"So there probably isn't a whole network of passageways. Dr. Hackman must have had them built only where he'd need them."

"Where would he need them?"

"That's what we have to figure out. Obviously he wanted to be able to go back and forth from his library to his office without anyone noticing."

"Why?"

"I don't know. The guy liked secrets. Remember?"

"He must have been weird."

"Maybe he planned to hide things in the passageways and just didn't get around to it," Jeff said.

"Or maybe he wanted to be able to spy on people," Debbie said.

"What people?"

"He was going to turn the house into a museum."

"That's right. So, if the house was full of people looking at the stuff in his museum, where else would he want to go in his passageways to stay out of their way?"

"To the kitchen, when he was hungry," Debbie said. She reached for her camera case. "I'm starving. Can't we eat some of the sandwiches now?"

At the mention of food, Jeff's stomach rumbled.

"I take that as an answer," she said. She opened the case and pulled out two sandwiches, handing one of them to Jeff.

"Did you bring a watch?" Jeff mumbled as he bit into a cheese sandwich.

"No. I wonder what time it is," Debbie said.

Jeff finished his sandwich in a few gulps, wiped his mouth with the back of his hand, and stood up. "It's getting darker," he said.

Debbie joined him at the window. "The storm isn't letting up a bit."

"It's a bad one."

"Grandma said it would be. We should have listened to her." She sighed, and added, "Want another sandwich?"

"No," Jeff said. "We'd better save as much of the food as we can."

"How about a cookie? Would that be all right?" Debbie reached into her coat pocket and fished out a crumbled chocolate cookie, dropping the pieces into Jeff's hand along with some lint and a piece of torn Kleenex.

"Yuck," he said. "Nobody'd want to eat this mess."

"I would. I'm hungry," Debbie said. She picked the cookie pieces from his hand and popped them into her mouth.

"I bet I know where there's a passage," Jeff said. "There must be one to the bedroom in the back tower."

Debbie stopped munching and stared at him. "Why?"

"Because someone got into that room too easily. Someone came in while Paul Karsten was sleeping and opened the windows. He might not have climbed the stairs. There might have been a secret way."

"We don't have to look there, do we?"

"Yes, we do. It's our best chance, so far. And now would be a good time, before it gets dark."

"I'm not going to like it," Debbie said.

"Don't stop to think about whether you'll like it or not. Let's just go there — now!"

Debbie scooped up her camera case and followed Jeff into the entry hall. "I'll just take my camera with me. I don't want to carry this case everywhere we go," Debbie said. She put the case on the chair next to her flashlight.

They climbed the stairs, carefully avoiding the places where the railing was broken and wobbly, and quietly walked down the upstairs hallway until they came to a narrow door. "You came to this spot just like you've been here before," Debbie said, as Jeff opened the door to a narrow, twisting stairway.

"I was paying attention to Mr. Karsten's story." He peered up the stairs. "Want to go first? Or last?"

Debbie looked behind her. "Neither, but I suppose if I have to, I'll be first. I don't want something creeping up behind me."

"I wish you wouldn't say dumb things like that!" Jeff shouted. He let her climb the stairs first, but he edged up sideways, one eye on the stairs behind them. It was dim on the stairway, but they could see, because the door to the tower room stood open.

Jeff followed Debbie into the room. Automatically he shut the door and turned the key. It grated in the lock, but it did turn. He leaned against the door with relief.

The room looked as Mr. Karsten had described it, except that the middle window was broken. Snow was piled on the floor under it, and years of winter weather and rain had badly stained the walls and floors. A small rag rug was in tatters, and the bedspread looked so dirty and flimsy that Jeff thought a puff of air might cause it to disintegrate.

He knew the gold coin with the eyes and the jackal head couldn't possibly be in the room, but just to play it safe he opened the drawers in the chest. Nothing was there, except one long, black stocking and a yellowed copy of *Tip Top Weekly*.

"Frank Merriwell," Jeff murmured. He pulled out the magazine, rolled it, and tucked it into one of his coat pockets. He shivered. This was a part of Mr. Karsten's story, and the story had become very real.

"Thump on the walls. Maybe one of them will sound hollow," Debbie said.

They rapped on the walls and poked and pushed,

but nothing moved, and all the tapping noises sounded the same.

"I think you were wrong," Debbie said, dusting off her hands. "Let's go back. It's really getting a lot darker now. We need our flashlights."

"I've got mine." Jeff turned it on, but there was only a faint glow. "Darn!" he said. "I thought Mom would have put new batteries in it! Where are the extra batteries?"

"Downstairs in the entry hall in my camera case." She gave him an apologetic smile. "Next to my flashlight."

"We'd better get them right now," Jeff said, as he snapped off his flashlight. He had one hand on the doorknob and one hand on the key, ready to turn it, when they heard measured footsteps slowly coming toward them, up the stairs!

12

Who's there?" Jeff croaked, and it frightened him even more to know he was following so closely the story Mr. Karsten had told them.

The footsteps stopped.

Jeff remembered the little desk chair. Trying to tiptoe, but stumbling and tripping, Jeff grabbed the chair and quickly shoved it under the doorknob of the door, making sure it was wedged tightly.

Again there was silence, until a board on the stairs creaked, and the slow footsteps began again.

Neither Jeff nor Debbie moved as the footsteps came closer and closer, then stopped outside the door.

There was a pause, as though someone was listening. Then a light scratching began on the other side of the door.

Debbie gasped. Jeff's knees wobbled. He backed

up and plopped down on the bed, sending up a cloud of dust.

He knew Debbie was going to say it, and he shuddered, knowing what the answer would be.

"What do you want?" Debbie whispered.

And a voice whispered back, "Where are my eyes?"

Debbie let out a yelp and began shouting, "How should we know? We didn't take your eyes! What do you think you're doing anyway, going around scaring people? You rotten, mean, whatever-you-are!"

Jeff jumped up and grabbed Debbie, shaking her as the doorknob rattled. "Stop that!" he whispered. "You're just making him mad."

The door groaned against its hinges. "We've got to get out of here!" Debbie said.

"How?" Jeff looked at the windows. The gusts of snow and the darkness hid the cliff below, but they knew it was there. They couldn't escape from the window. He shifted the flashlight in his hand. It wasn't very heavy, but maybe he could use it to help defend them.

"We should hide," Debbie said. Frantically she looked around the room. "We can hide in the wardrobe!"

Debbie threw open the doors to the wardrobe and tugged on Jeff's arm. "We'll just be trapped in here," he said, trying to pull free from Debbie's grip.

Debbie was already inside the wardrobe. As hard as she could, Debbie yanked on Jeff's arm, throwing him off balance. He fell into the wardrobe on top of her, bumping his chin on her camera and slamming against the back wall.

The back panel suddenly cracked and split, and Jeff found himself falling, in a tangle with Debbie's arms and legs, until he landed with a thump. Debbie was lying on top of him, his flashlight pressed into his backbone, and his head was wedged against a wall.

He pulled Debbie's elbow out of his mouth and whispered, "Debbie? Are you hurt?"

"I'm okay. What happened?" Debbie tried to sit up and said, "Ouch! The ceiling's low. Don't bump your head."

It was too dark to see. Jeff explored the floor with one hand. "Hey," he said, "we're on some kind of stairway."

"Another passageway!" Debbie said. "I bet it's under the other stairway."

"If you'll get off me we could crawl down," Jeff said.

Puffing and grunting, Debbie managed to climb over Jeff, turning around so that she could back down the stairs. "Okay," she said, "follow me, but

91

not too closely. I don't want your feet in my face."

The narrow stairs twisted tightly, so the going was slow. At one point Debbie stopped and said, "Wait a minute! What if the mummy's hidden in here? What if we bump into it?"

"Don't even think like that!" Jeff snapped. "Keep going!"

Finally Jeff's foot touched something, and Debbie said, "Ouch! Get your foot off my head!"

"Why did you stop this time?"

"Because there's a wall or a door or something blocking the way."

"Push on it!" Jeff said.

"How do we know what's on the other side?"

"Would you rather go back to the tower room?" Jeff asked. "We don't have much choice, do we?"

Jeff could hear Debbie squirming around, grunting and muttering to herself. "What are you doing?" he whispered.

At that moment Debbie said, "Ha! I found it! I knew there would be a latch some place!"

Jeff heard a scraping noise, and Debbie whispered, "Well? What are you waiting for? The door's open!"

He scrambled down the remaining stairs and found himself in some kind of box with soft things brushing against his head. He reached up an arm to protect himself and discovered he had a handful of what felt like clothes.

"Climb out," Debbie said. "You're in another wardrobe."

Jeff edged backward and got to his feet, shaking himself and brushing himself off. He turned on his flashlight, and there was enough light from the faint glow to outline a high, carved, canopied bed, and a wide armchair. Beside the large wardrobe stood a massive chest of drawers. Another chair and table were placed under the window across the room. The top of the chest and the table were cluttered with things. Jeff recognized the shape of a few ornate picture frames and a dusty pair of wire-rimmed eyeglasses, but the rest seemed to be mostly small vases and bowls and little figures.

"I bet this was Dr. Hackman's bedroom," Debbie said.

"Then those must have been his clothes in the wardrobe," Jeff said. "Dr. Hackman wouldn't have left without taking his clothes with him. But how could he just disappear?"

"I think Anubis scared him away," Debbie said. "He was probably so frightened he ran and ran and never came back."

"No," Jeff said. "He wouldn't leave all the things he'd collected and his plans for a museum. It meant too much to him."

"If he didn't go away from here, he'd still have to be here," Debbie said. She gave a little screech.

"Oh, no! Don't say things like that, Jeff! You scared me!"

"You're the one who said it, not me."

"Well, you made me think it!" She sighed. "Have you changed your mind? Do you believe Mr. Karsten's story now?"

"I don't know what to believe," Jeff said. He shuddered. "All I know is that someone — or something — is in the house with us."

The light from the flashlight faded completely. Jeff dropped the flashlight into his coat pocket and said, "We'll have to get the other flashlight and the batteries that you left downstairs."

Debbie's voice spoke near his ear. "How are we going to find our way downstairs? It's so dark!"

"First of all," Jeff said, as he bumped into the wardrobe, banging his knee, "we'll find the door. We know what direction it's in."

"Okay," Debbie said. "Let me hang onto you." She took his hand, and he inched his way across the room until his toes touched the wall. It was just a matter of minutes until he found the door, then the doorknob. Before he swung the door open he whispered, "Let's figure this out. Judging from the direction we took on the hidden stairs, Dr. Hackman's room must be just about under the tower room. That means the door to the stairway to the tower is very close to us — probably a little to the right. So don't say a word. We don't want anything — uh — anybody to hear us."

Debbie clutched Jeff's hand tightly. He quietly opened the door and edged into the hallway. Debbie moved against him, and he thought he could hear her heart thumping. Maybe it was his own. It was the only sound he could hear. The house was silent.

Jeff stretched out his right hand and guided himself along the wall in the direction of the stairway that led to the entrance hall. It seemed to take forever, especially since they stopped every few feet to listen. Apparently whatever had tried to get into the tower room was not following them.

The tattered drapes that still hung over the windows above the entry hall managed to cut out whatever light might have come from outside. Jeff strained to see through the darkness inside the house, but he could make out only a few shadows and shapes.

Jeff stopped and whispered to Debbie, "I need to find the railing, so we'll know if we're near the stairway. I'll have to cross the hall."

"I'll go with you."

"No," he whispered. "You stay here. That railing is wobbly. I don't want to take any chances of either of us falling over the edge."

He pulled his hand away from hers and walked carefully across the hallway, arms outstretched.

His fingers finally touched the railing, which

moved slightly. He backed off a step. The head of the stairs should be just a few feet beyond.

A hand slipped into his, clutching his fingers so tightly they felt numb. Jeff whispered, "Don't you do anything anyone tells you, Debbie? You were supposed to stay back against the wall! And don't squeeze my hand so hard. It hurts!"

She didn't answer, just pressed close to him as he worked his way toward what he hoped would be the head of the stairs. Finally he touched a wall, and stretched out his left foot. Just as he thought, he was on the top step.

"Okay," he murmured to Debbie. "We're at the head of the stairs. We'll reach the flashlight and batteries in no time."

His left foot was poised above the first step down when he heard a hiss from across the hallway.

"Hey, Jeff!" Debbie called in a loud whisper, "I'm scared here all alone! Where are you?"

Jeff opened his mouth to answer her, but nothing came out. If Debbie was still waiting for him against the wall, then who — or what — was holding his hand?

13

Jeff couldn't move. He couldn't breathe. Someone was gripping his hand, and obviously it
wasn't Debbie!

Debbie called out again, terror in her voice.
"Jeff! Why don't you answer me?" She made a
squeaking sound, like a mouse with a cat after it,
and whimpered, "I'll have to find him, I guess."

"No! Stay there!" Jeff threw himself backward, jerking his hand from the grasp of those
unknown fingers. He pulled himself into a ball,
falling, bumping, and sliding down the stairs, until he landed flat on the floor of the entry hall.
Every inch of his body ached, but he pulled himself to his knees, crawling and scrambling as fast
as he could in the direction of the chair that held
Grandma's flashlight.

He banged into a leg of the chair, groped for the
flashlight, found it, and quickly turned it on.

The strong beam swept upward along the
stairway. Nothing was there.

"Debbie!" Jeff yelled. "Can you see the light?"

She appeared at the top of the stairs. "Get down here fast!" he shouted. "Hurry!"

Debbie ran down the stairs, crying, "Where were you, Jeffrey Scott? Why didn't you answer me? What were you doing, trying to scare me like that? Do you know how scared I was waiting there in that — "

She had reached the bottom of the stairs, and Jeff grabbed her arm. "Be quiet," he said. "Hold this light." He dumped the old batteries from his flashlight and fished new ones from the camera case, his fingers fumbling as he hurried. And while he worked he told her about the hand that had been holding his.

Debbie gasped. "How could you stand it? I'm glad it didn't happen to me! I would have died, right there on the stairs, and you would have had to drag my body all the way down." Her eyes grew even wider, and she looked in the direction of the stairs. "Where is he now?" she whispered to Jeff.

"I don't know," he said, "but we're going to find out pretty soon." He tested his flashlight by shining it against the statues on the table, and the beam was strong.

"What do you mean?" Debbie moved closer to him.

"I mean," he said, "that we're going to trap whoever or whatever it is."

"Did your brains bounce out while you were falling down stairs?"

"Think about it," he said. "Wouldn't you feel a lot safer in this house if he's locked up where he can't get to us?"

She studied him from the corners of her eyes. "Locked up where? And how?"

Jeff put his mouth close to Debbie's ear, hoping he wouldn't be overheard. "I think our answer is in the statue of Anubis."

Debbie jumped.

"Don't do that!" Jeff grumbled, pulling a strand of her hair from his mouth. "Hold still and listen. I'm going to find out if that gold coin is still in the base of the statue. If it is, then we've got a plan."

"What plan?" she whispered.

"We're going to lure whoever was on the stairs into the library."

"Oh, c'mon, Jeff," she said, pulling away. "We lure him into the library? How do we do that? Promise to read to him?"

"Just listen to what I have in mind," Jeff said. "Remember the passageway between the library and the office? I want you to hide in the office, just inside the door. Turn off your flashlight when you get there. I'll put the coin on one of the book-shelves in the library, then climb in the passage-way, and join you in the office. If the whatever-it-is goes after the coin, we can lock both the library and office doors. He won't be able to get out."

"Are you sure? If he has the coin he'll have all his powers."

"He had those powers anyway, because the coin was in the statue, and he still couldn't get through the locked door in the tower room."

Debbie sighed. "I guess it's better than waiting to see what he'll do next."

As Debbie held the beam of the flashlight on the table, Jeff put his flashlight down carefully and picked up the statue of Anubis. It was warm to his touch, frightening Jeff so much that he nearly dropped it. But as quickly as he could he fumbled with the base of the statue, finally managing to pry it off.

A triangular-shaped gold coin clattered to the table top, and at the same time a sharp cry came from the landing above their heads.

"Run, Debbie!" As Debbie raced out of the room, Jeff snatched up the coin and his flashlight and dashed toward the library. He placed the coin on a shelf opposite the door, then scrambled into the cupboard under the window, shutting the cupboard door with shaking fingers.

The passage was short, and the flashlight helped him find his way so, in what seemed like just a few seconds, Jeff burst into the office.

Now it was Debbie's turn to hush him. "Be

quiet," she whispered as she peered out of the doorway. "I think something's coming!"

Jeff joined Debbie and waited. Soft footsteps seemed to come down the stairs, across the entry hall, and into the hallway. He held his breath, straining to see, wondering if there was anything there to see.

Debbie's fingers dug into his arm. He heard her sharp intake of breath before he saw the figure poised before the open door to the library.

It was as tall as a man with the body of a man, but its head was that of a jackal. Its long ears twitched as though aware of every sound.

Jeff didn't dare to move until the figure disappeared into the library. Then, trying not to panic, he elbowed Debbie aside and with all his strength made a dash for the library door and locked it. The key was stiff in the lock, and for a frantic moment Jeff struggled and grunted and was afraid he couldn't budge it. Just as he felt a pull on the other side of the doorknob, the key twisted into place, and the door was firmly locked.

Jeff leaned against the wall with a sigh of relief. "We did it!" he said to Debbie.

"If we could only leave now and go to Grandpa's house," Debbie said.

They could hear heavy breathing on the other side of the door, and thumps against the heavy wood.

Debbie edged away from the door. "Let's go back to the entry hall," she whispered.

Gladly Jeff followed her. They sat on chairs near the front door. Debbie turned off her flashlight, and Jeff idly let the beam from his travel over the pictures and tapestries on the walls and over the carved letters on the archway. The light cut deep shadows in the carvings. In one place the shadows were strangely deeper and darker.

"Look at that, Debbie!" Jeff said.

"I've seen it," Debbie grumbled. "Dr. Hackman and his dumb secrets."

Jeff got to his feet, his light still trained on the carving. "No, I mean look at the words: 'ONLY I KNOW THE SECRET.' Do you see something different about the 'I'?"

Debbie jumped up and stood next to him. "It seems to have a deeper shadow. But what about it?"

"I wonder," Jeff said. He walked to the archway and looked up, then dragged over a nearby chair and stood on it, reaching upward.

"Too short," he said. "Help me move the table over there."

"That big table?" Debbie asked.

"What other table? Come on. We can do it. It should slide right across the floor."

"What about the statues on it?"

"I'll put them on the floor against the wall,

where they won't get hurt." Quickly, as Debbie held the flashlight so he could see, Jeff placed the statues in a neat row against the wall. Then he and Debbie shoved and pushed and pulled until the table was under the arch.

"I think I can reach now," Jeff said. "Shine your light on the letter 'ı.' " He climbed on the table and stretched to his limit, but couldn't touch the arch; so he hopped down to the floor. "We'll have to put one of the chairs up there," he added.

"What is this all about?" Debbie asked, as she helped him lift one of the chairs to the table top. "What are you trying to do?"

"Uncover Dr. Hackman's secret," Jeff said. He set the chair under the arch and climbed on it. It creaked and wobbled.

Debbie grabbed the nearest chair leg and tried to support it.

Jeff carefully balanced himself and reached upward. He held onto the arch for support as the chair wiggled. "Debbie," he said, "I think Dr. Hackman carved a hiding place for himself up here."

"In the 'ı'?" She answered her own question. "That's really clever. The 'ı' knows the secret."

Jeff's fingers groped back into the carving more deeply than he had imagined. There was a hole gouged out, cut from the wood below the letter. He felt some tightly folded papers, which he fished out and stuffed into one of his pockets. Finally, at the bottom of the hole, his fingertips touched something smooth and icy cold.

Instinctively he jerked back. Then, holding his breath, he reached in as far as he could, caught the object between his first two fingers, and pulled it upward. By the time he had it in his hand he knew what it was. His guess had been right!

He held it out for Debbie to see and laughed. "What better place to find the mummy's eyes than in another 'I'?"

Debbie's flashlight wavered. "Jeff! You found the mummy's eyes! You really did! We'll get the reward!"

Jeff jumped from the chair to the table top and from the table top to the floor. "No," he said. "The reward is for finding the mummy, although I'm sure the Egyptian museum will be glad to get these eyes."

A long, angry cry came from the direction of the library.

Debbie shivered and said, "I think someone else wants them, too!"

14

Forget him," Jeff said. "He's locked up." But he turned so that the hallway wasn't at his back.

While Debbie held the golden eyes, running her fingers over the cold metal, Jeff pulled the papers from his pocket and examined them.

"Bank papers, accounts and stuff," he said as he opened some of the papers and folded them up again. He shook out a larger piece of paper and whistled.

"What are you looking at?" Debbie craned to see over his shoulder.

"It's a layout of the house," he said.

Debbie grabbed one side of the paper. "Look!" she said, "there's the passageway between the library and the office."

"And the secret stairway to the tower room," Jeff said. He looked carefully at the drawings of both floors. "That's it. No more passageways. Funny. I thought the house would be full of them."

"What's this?" Debbie pointed to a drawing at the right lower corner of the paper.

Jeff studied it. "The basement, of course." He began to get excited. "There's the alcove Mr. Karsten told us about!"

Jeff suddenly had an idea, but he wasn't sure how Debbie would take it. "Hey, Debbie," he said, "you want to get some really good pictures for your camera club entry, don't you?"

But Debbie wasn't paying attention to him. She held up a hand. "Be quiet. Listen!"

Jeff did. He couldn't hear a thing, not even a sound from the library. "What did you hear?" he whispered.

"Nothing," she said.

"What?"

"Nothing at all! No wind, no storm! I just realized that the storm must have been over at least an hour or so ago!"

They ran to the front door and opened it. Only a few flakes were falling, but the snow was deep, mounding over the porch steps. Clouds still covered the moon, and it was impossible to see anything past the spots of light made by their flashlights.

Debbie gave a happy sigh. "We can go home as soon as it's light!" She handed Jeff the golden eyes, and he dropped them into his pocket.

Jeff had no idea how much time was left before

dawn. Urgently he said, "Debbie, listen to me. We may not have much time left in this house, and there's still something to do!"

She shivered and shut the door, turning to look at him with suspicion. "Let me guess," she said. "Could this possibly have to do with a mummy? No, no, that's too ridiculous."

"Come on, Debbie," he said. "You know the only reason we came here was to try to find that mummy and get the reward."

"You found the eyes."

"So that ought to prove that the mummy is somewhere around. There's one place we haven't looked, and I think we ought to."

"Don't say it!" She backed away from him. "You want to look in the basement, don't you?"

Jeff shrugged. "It's logical, isn't it?" Before she could answer, he said, "We've got Anubis locked up. He can't get out to harm us. And it won't take more than a few minutes to look around the basement. Besides, think about that camera you want. You can get it if we find the mummy."

Debbie thought a moment. "I don't like the idea. Remember, when Mr. Karsten's mother called the police they came and searched. They would have seen the mummy if it was in the basement!"

"Maybe it was hidden in some way. I just have a feeling that as long as we're here we should investigate the basement." Jeff paused and then added, "That reward means a lot to me."

"Well. . . ."

Jeff picked up Debbie's camera and handed it to her. "If you have a picture of a mummy, you might win your camera club contest, too."

She turned one of her pockets inside out, emptying it of cookie crumbs. She reached into the camera case and pulled out a pack of film, stuffing it into the pocket, then hung the camera strap over her wrist. "I suppose you want to go down there right now," she said.

Jeff was so eager he ran to the basement door.

"Remember the doorstop!" Debbie said as she rushed to catch up with him.

It was still in the hallway, against the door. Debbie picked it up and shoved it into place as Jeff opened the door. "Everything in this house is still just where it was," she whispered. "I feel at times as though we've walked right into Mr. Karsten's story. I keep waiting for something awful to happen to us."

"Don't get crazy ideas," Jeff said quickly, not wanting to admit that he had the same feelings. He aimed the beam of his flashlight at the cement steps. "Stick close to the wall," he told her. "We can't trust the handrail."

They both made sure that the doorstop would keep the door from closing, then slowly made their way down the stairs.

As they reached the bottom of the stairs they stopped and directed their flashlights around the brick walls of the basement. At the near end there were shelves that were cluttered with small tools and rope and things usually found in basements. Against the walls were a number of large crates and boxes.

"It's bigger than I thought it would be," Debbie said. "Anything could be hiding down here!"

"Don't think like that. You'll just scare yourself."

"I'm already scared!"

"Well, don't scare *me* them!"

Shadows leaped and jumped as their flashlights moved over the things stored in the basement. Jeff shuddered.

"I wonder what's in the boxes," Debbie said. "There's no telling what might be inside. All sorts of weird and creepy stuff, I bet."

"I'm going to stuff you in one of them if you don't quit that!" Jeff said. He turned and walked toward the right side of the basement. Debbie nearly stumbled in her eagerness to catch up with him. "I tripped on something," she said.

"Watch where you're going," Jeff answered.

"I am watching. It looks like a square. There are lines in the floor. Come and look at it. What is it?"

Jeff turned back and joined her. He followed the

beam of her flashlight. Under the heavy layer of dust on the cement floor was the outline of a square. One edge of the square was slightly raised. "Is that what you tripped on?" he asked.

"I guess. You know what I think it is? A trap door."

Jeff pulled out the diagram. "So that's what that means," he said. "There's a square drawn right here, but it's not labeled."

"If it's a door, does it open?"

"We can find out."

They stopped to feel around it, and Debbie asked, "Where's the screwdriver you brought? This door is made of wood, and I don't think it's as thick as it looks. I bet we could pry it up."

Jeff tugged the screwdriver from his coat pocket and managed to wedge it into the place that was slightly raised. Using it as a lever he raised the door. They got their fingers under it and pulled it all the way open.

Below them was an open cavelike room that seemed to be cut from rock.

"I'll see what that is," Jeff said, and he dropped into the room. The floor was only about four feet from the opening, so it was easy. He aimed his flashlight ahead of him and could see that the roof quickly became higher, so he could stand. There were two large metal rings bolted to the ceiling near the door, with a rod resting in them. Apparently it was some kind of a bolt to keep the trap door fastened from this side.

Jeff followed the path of his light about ten feet until it abruptly stopped. He blinked and strained to see, and finally realized he was looking out at a sky that was just beginning to change from dark to dawn. Below him he could make out a few steps. There was a kind of landing about six feet below the cave, and from there a set of steps went straight down, toward the valley. Another went upward to the side, and he guessed they would end at the top of the hill, on the side of the house. He shone the light overhead and saw what looked like the roof of a cave.

Debbie's head appeared in the opening. "What did you find?" she called.

Jeff jumped and caught the edge of the opening, pulling himself up and into the basement.

He told Debbie what he had seen, and she said, "Mr. Karsten told us about the steps in the cliff. They must have led from the cave. What do you suppose Dr. Hackman used them for?"

"Maybe a quick getaway," Jeff said. "We'll never know, will we?" He closed the trap door carefully and headed for the brick wall again.

He stopped and shone his light on the wall. "That's funny," he said. "The alcove isn't here where it's supposed to be. Hold my flashlight while I look at that diagram again."

He looked at the diagram, then at the wall. "That's weird," he said. "Mr. Karsten told us about an alcove with the mummy in it, and the diagram shows an alcove, but look at that wall." He pointed straight ahead. "In that spot is where the alcove should be, but it's just not there!"

Jeff walked along the wall, lightly running his fingers over it. He turned and walked back, poking at the mortar between the bricks and bending to examine it closely.

"Now what are you doing?" Debbie asked.

He stood, rubbing his thumb and forefinger together. "Look at this stuff crumble," he said. "It's not like the mortar that's holding the bricks in the rest of the wall. I think this section was done later."

"You mean someone walled over the alcove?"

Jeff was getting excited. "Yes! So the mummy might still be there!"

"How will we find out?"

Jeff tugged the screwdriver out of his pocket. "I knew this would come in handy," he said.

He turned off his flashlight, and Debbie trained hers on the wall, as he chipped at the mortar with the screwdriver. Chunks of it crumbled and fell on the other side of the wall.

Finally he was able to pull out two of the bricks. A third one dropped and smashed on the floor, just missing his feet. He worked faster now, until he had made a hole large enough to see into.

Debbie shone the light inside the hole, and let out a shriek.

"It's really there!" Jeff shouted. "I found the mummy!" He stared at the painted designs on the bindings that wrapped the mummy, scarcely able to believe his good luck. He had found it. He'd tell the people at the bank where the mummy could be found, and the reward would be his!

He worked even faster to chip away the mortar and make a large hole. He didn't think a mummy would be very heavy. Maybe he and Debbie could carry it out of the alcove. He hammered with the screwdriver and tugged away the bricks, until Debbie put a hand on his shoulder.

"Stop a minute, Jeff," she said.

He straightened. "I want to finish this, Debbie. I'm almost to the floor, and pretty soon we'll be able to get into the alcove and get the mummy out of there."

"And his friend," she said.

"What?"

"Take a look in that alcove," Debbie said. "There are *two* mummies."

Jeff peered inside the large hole he had made. To one side of the small alcove was a second mummy, propped upright against the wall.

Debbie took a picture of the mummies while Jeff held the flashlight. "That's a sloppy one," she said.

"He's lumpy and bumpy and isn't even painted, and those wrappings are a mess. Look — up at the top of his head — that piece of cloth is loose, just hanging there."

She reached into the alcove and grabbed the end of the cloth. "See what I mean?" she said.

Apparently Debbie pulled on the cloth harder than she had meant to, because a section of the wrappings came apart in her hand, falling from the head.

Jeff stared into a dried, shriveled, gray-bearded face that seemed to be peering at him from under a faded blue yachting cap.

Debbie screamed in his ear. The flashlight bounced on the floor, its light flicking back and forth on the mummies, making them seem like characters in a strobe show. "It's Dr. Hackman, isn't it?" she yelled.

Jeff struggled to maintain calm, shouting, "Stop it, Debbie! Calm down! We can't panic! We've got to think of what to do next!"

"I want to get out of this basement!"

"Okay. Stop jumping around, and we will."

Debbie stood still and stared at Jeff. "Right now?"

"Right now!" he answered, trying to keep his teeth from chattering.

But at that moment, with a thud, someone shut the basement door.

15

Debbie grabbed for her flashlight and the picture of the mummies. Jeff pulled his flashlight out, flicking it on. At the same time they ran toward the foot of the stairs, shining their lights at the door. The door was firmly closed.

"Anubis?" Debbie whispered.

"I don't understand how he could have got out," Jeff said. "I locked the library door, and you locked the door to the office."

"Correction," Debbie said. "You locked both the doors."

Jeff stared at her. "No, I didn't. You were supposed to lock the office door while I locked the library door."

"You didn't tell me that. You just said we'd lock the doors. You pushed me into the hall when you ran out of the office. I thought you locked the office door, too."

Jeff groaned. "He must have found the passageway and got out. I'm sorry, Debbie."

She tried to smile. "It's okay," she said. "We're the gruesome twosome, aren't we? We'll figure something out."

Jeff hefted the screwdriver in his hand. "Let me see what I can do with this. I bet I can chip away the wood around the lock, or even use this to press back the lock. I'm going to try."

One silent step at a time Jeff went up the stairs. Debbie followed him.

Jeff held up a hand. They both stood without moving, listening, wondering if Anubis was on the other side of the door.

It didn't take long to find out. There was a soft, animal-like snuffling at the edge of the door.

Jeff held a finger to his lips, then motioned Debbie to follow him down the stairs. When they reached the foot of the stairs he whispered, "We don't want to go out that way! We'll use the trap door. Come on. Help me lift it."

Again he used the screwdriver to help pry the door open. They laid it back as silently as they could. Jeff dropped to the floor of the cave and put down his flashlight, the beam turned on.

"Move over," Debbie whispered. "I'm coming down."

"Not yet." Jeff hoisted himself back onto the basement floor. "You have to help me carry the mummy down there!"

"Your brain has melted and run out your ears! We can't get the mummy down there!"

Jeff put a hand on her arm. "Listen, Debbie. This is important. We've found the mummy. We can't just leave it here."

"Oh, yes we can!"

"The thing is dried and it won't weigh as much as a live person. We could carry it easy. Come on. Help me do it."

Debbie glanced up at the basement door. "What about Anubis?"

"He's just waiting there for us to try to get out. We can carry the mummy into the cave and bolt the door, and Anubis won't know anything about it."

She scowled as she thought, and Jeff quickly added, "I have to get that reward for my father. Okay, Debbie? This will be the very last thing I'll ask you to do in my entire life."

Debbie shuddered, but she got to her feet. "That's what I'm afraid of."

Jeff climbed into the alcove, shivering as he brushed against Dr. Hackman's mummy. Debbie tucked her flashlight under her chin, put her camera strap over her wrist, and grabbed the Egyptian mummy's feet, pulling them outward. Jeff balanced his head. "See — he's not that heavy," he whispered.

Taking one careful step at a time, they made their way across the floor, heading toward the trap door.

"Jeff, I just thought of something awful!" Debbie grunted, her chin pressed against the flashlight. "Maybe Anubis isn't planning to wait for us to come up the stairs. Maybe he's going to come down here and do to us what he did to Dr. Hackman!"

"Keep moving," Jeff said.

"I think we should just put this mummy down right here and get out of this place as fast as we can!"

They were below the stairs now, and Debbie twisted her neck so that the flashlight shone upward, toward the door to the basement.

"I said, 'Don't stop!' " But Jeff automatically glanced upward. The door to the basement was opening.

As they watched, the strange figure of a man with the head of a jackal appeared on the top stair. He gave a sharp cry that sounded almost like a laugh.

"He's coming!" Debbie shrieked, and her flashlight bounced to the floor.

"Don't drop the mummy!" Jeff yelled. "We're almost there!"

He pushed, and Debbie responded. Stumbling, nearly falling, they reached the open trap door.

The beam from the flashlight illuminated the stairway enough so that Jeff could see Anubis coming down the stairs toward them.

"Jump down!" Jeff shouted to Debbie.

As she dropped through the trap door she cried, "Leave the mummy! Get in here, Jeff!"

Anubis had almost reached the bottom stair. Jeff tilted the mummy into the hole. "Grab his feet and pull!" he yelled.

"I am pulling!" Debbie called back. "He's stuck! He won't fit through this space!"

Anubis laughed his horrible cry again, and the sound echoed throughout the basement. He was moving closer to Jeff, but slowly, as though he knew there was no way they could escape him.

Jeff, still clutching the mummy's shoulders, turned and stared right into Anubis' dark, gleaming eyes!

16

J eff screamed, "Push the mummy back up here, Debbie!" He frantically tugged with all his strength, and the mummy came loose and shot upward. Anubis, teeth bared, lunged toward Jeff. But Jeff, with a super strength he knew came only from his terror, shoved the mummy between them, and threw it at Anubis. The weird half man, half jackal automatically clutched the painted figure and staggered backward.

Jeff grabbed the trap door, pulling it after him as he dropped through. He slammed the iron bar through the rings, locking it in place. Then he dropped to the floor and rested his head on his knees, hugging them tightly until he stopped shaking.

The door rattled above his head and they could hear Anubis' furious cry.

Jeff felt Debbie's hand on his shoulder. "Are you okay?" she asked. He nodded, and she stared at the door over their heads, adding, "He can't get through, can he?"

"I doubt it," Jeff said.

"Have you noticed something?" Debbie asked. "It's light. It's morning!"

Jeff managed to get to his feet. His legs still wobbled, but he was able to walk to the edge of the cave. Below them the valley glistened in the early sunlight.

"Where are the steps?" Debbie asked.

Jeff leaned out and pointed. "There's a landing just below the cave. They start at the landing."

Debbie sat down, rolled on her stomach, and dangled her feet over the edge of the cave floor. "How much farther down is it?" she grunted.

"You can do it," Jeff said. "The drop is only about six feet."

Debbie dropped, staggered a bit, and leaned against the side of the cliff. "No big deal," she said. "Come on."

It took Jeff just a minute to join her. He glanced back at the entrance to the cave. "I hope Anubis doesn't hurt the mummy! I wish we'd been able to get it down here!"

"Forget the mummy!" Debbie said. "We've got to get out of here!"

The steps were slippery from the snow, but there were handholds, and they crawled slowly and carefully. The ancient house loomed above them.

"We can go down to the valley," Debbie said, "or up, around to the front of the house." She shuddered.

"There's too much snow on the steps," Jeff said. "Our best chance is up. It's a lot shorter."

"But what if we find Anubis waiting for us there?"

"Don't even think about it," Jeff told her. "Just keep moving."

They climbed, struggling and slipping, not daring to look upward, concentrating on grabbing bushes and fists of shrubs to make the going easier. Soon the brick walls of the house crowded against them, and the steps became narrower; but finally they reached a gentle slope and were able to stand upright.

"We're at the top," Jeff said.

They heard the grinding of a motor and a whooshing noise. It seemed to be near and coming toward them.

They tried to run toward the source of the sound, sinking into the snow with each step, falling and scrambling until they rounded the corner of the house and stood in front of the porch, looking down the hill and down the drive. A snowplow, spitting clouds of snow to the side, was lumbering up the hill.

They jumped and waved and hurried toward it. Someone next to the driver leaned out, snow flying over his head, and waved back. It was Grandpa! Grandpa jumped from the snowplow and ran toward them. Someone else jumped, too, and Jeff was surprised to see that it was Mr. Karsten.

Jeff found himself swept off his feet as he and Debbie were wrapped in a strong hug.

"Mr. Karsten was afraid you had come here!" Grandpa said.

"We should have told you, I know," Jeff began, but Grandpa held up a hand.

"You're in a lot of trouble with your grandma," he said, "but for now, I'm just grateful we found you!"

The snowplow driver ran toward the house, shouting over the roar of the motor, "Mr. Karsten went in there! And the place is on fire! Help me find him!"

Jeff turned toward the Hackman house, so shocked that for a few moments he couldn't move. Black smoke was pouring through the broken front windows. Orange flame was devouring the draperies at the entry hall.

"Mr. Karsten!" he yelled. Then he was running, too.

But before they reached the front porch Mr. Karsten stumbled from the house. "Move back!" he shouted.

They staggered through the deep snow until they were at a safe distance from the house.

"Shouldn't we call the fire department?" Debbie asked as they watched the house burn. They could hear crashing sounds as well as the crackle of the flames as walls within the house crumbled and fell.

"Isn't there anything we can do?" Jeff asked.

Grandpa shook his head. "There's no way the volunteers could get here in time. The house is old and dry. It will burn fast."

"Small loss anyway," the driver said. "Folks will be glad that old haunted place is gone."

"It had to be put to rest," Mr. Karsten murmured, as though he were talking to himself, but Jeff heard him.

"Wonder how the house caught fire," the driver said.

No one answered him. Jeff knew, and he was sure that Grandpa and Debbie knew, too. He wished Mr. Karsten had only known about the mummy.

Jeff groaned. "The mummy was in there," he said. He looked at Mr. Karsten. "We found it."

The driver winked broadly. "Yeah? A real mummy. And you kids found it. My, my."

Debbie fumbled in her coat pockets and held up a snapshot. "We even took its picture," she said smugly. "By the way, that's Dr. Hackman's body next to the mummy."

The driver made a choking sound, and Grandpa's eyes widened. Mr. Karsten clutched the picture. He nodded and said, "It's over. At last it's over."

"But I wanted the reward for Dad," Jeff said. He fished the golden eyes from his pocket and gave them to Grandpa. "This is all I got — the mummy's eyes."

Grandpa gave a long whistle, and Mr. Karsten said, "I wouldn't worry about the mummy, if I were you, Jeff. There should be a fine reward for this!"

Jeff jumped as the roof of the house fell in with a crash. There'd be nothing left of the house and its memories but an ugly pile of rubble. The mummy was gone, and Anubis was gone. The horror would never return to Hackman's Hill.

Grandpa patted Jeff's shoulder. "Let's go home now. I want Grandma to know you're both safe, and we'll have to report to the fire department and the police."

They all climbed into the plow, squeezing together on the seat. "Mr. Karsten, Grandpa, we've got a lot to tell you!" Debbie shouted over the noise of the motor.

"Wait until we're home," Grandpa told her. "It's too noisy here. Besides, your grandma will want to hear the story, too. Of course, she may want to tell you our surprise first."

"What surprise?" Jeff asked.

"Remember?" Debbie yelled in his ear.

"Grandma told us that Grandpa was in town arranging a surprise for us."

"And I got the surprise! The tickets!" Grandpa shouted.

"Tickets?" Mr. Karsten suddenly exploded with laughter, clapping his hands in their heavy wool gloves over his mouth.

Grandpa looked surprised. "What's so funny about that?"

Mr. Karsten's eyes were twinkling. "The tickets are for the traveling museum show that's coming to the city. Isn't that right?"

"Yes," Grandpa said. "That special Egyptian show. We think Debbie and Jeff will be excited about seeing a real mummy."

The minute Grandpa realized what he had said, he began to roar with laughter. Jeff thought they should explain everything to the driver of the snowplow, who looked so puzzled at the way they were all acting. But he'd have to wait. Right now he couldn't stop laughing!